T. H. Passmore, M. A.

The Sacred Vestments

An English Rendering of the third book of the Rationale divinorum officiorum of

durandus, Bishop of Mende

T. H. Passmore, M. A.

The Sacred Vestments
An English Rendering of the third book of the Rationale divinorum officiorum of durandus, Bishop of Mende

ISBN/EAN: 9783741185335

Manufactured in Europe, USA, Canada, Australia, Japa

Cover: Foto ©Andreas Hilbeck / pixelio.de

Manufactured and distributed by brebook publishing software (www.brebook.com)

T. H. Passmore, M. A.

The Sacred Vestments

THE

SACRED VESTMENTS

AN ENGLISH RENDERING OF THE THIRD BOOK OF
THE 'RATIONALE DIVINORUM OFFICIORUM'
OF DURANDUS, BISHOP OF MENDE

WITH NOTES

BY THE

REV. T. H. PASSMORE, M.A.

LONDON
SAMPSON LOW, MARSTON & COMPANY
LIMITED
St. Dunstan's House
FETTER LANE, FLEET STREET, E.C.
1899

FOREWORD

WITH the exception of Neale and Webb's
'Symbolism,' which is an edited translation of
its first Book 'Of the Church and its Parts,' the
eight Books of the *Rationale Divinorum Officiorum* of Durandus have not, so far as I know,
been rendered into English. This means that
the greatest and most beautiful, perhaps, of
ancient works on the worship of the Catholic
Church is inaccessible to any but readers of
the Latin tongue.

What herein follows is an attempt in part to
supply this defect. In making it I have felt
that should the work fail to find readers (which
would appear unlikely in days when the mind
of all England is strained upon matters liturgical) the blame will attach to the inefficient
interpreter, not to the pious and gifted author,
of an illustrious book.

For the Catholic Revival, under God, in our

English Church has not yet brought us to that degree of liturgical perfection, that we can afford to turn a deaf ear to those great voices of the past which being dead yet speak to us of 'the sacred mysteries, and the virtues which they signify.' The lore of the sanctuary and the cunning of holy rite can hardly be called strong points with the English clergy, concede to them what we will of piety and reverence in heart. Nor is the cause far to seek, when we consider how sadly deficient is the ordinary course of English clerical training as regards that most necessary instruction in the externals of worship, without which it is impossible to enter with fitness upon the holiest of callings. The present writer may recall, without any invidious feeling whatever, the utter ignorance of the details of the offering of the Holy Sacrifice, in which he entered upon his ministry in the Church, after having received excellent instruction in both doctrinal and pastoral theology both at Cambridge and at one of the best of our Theological Colleges.

One has heard it put forth indeed almost

as a boast by many a good priest, that he is ' no
ritualist.' Yet it may be thought strange that
a craftsman should arrogate to himself either
ignorance or inefficiency in any department of
his craft, however subordinate, as a thing to be
vaunted. If ' Priestcraft,' which is the craft or
common business of a Priest, were less anathema-
tised and more studied, the Church would be a
gainer at large. Surely it is the solemn duty of
every Priest to be a ' Ritualist,' in so far as touches
the competent and careful discharge of his dread
office in the sanctuary. There is a tendency
even in Catholic minds, especially in times of
' Crisis '—which seem perennial—to think and
speak of Ritual a little slightingly, as though it
were the rival of interior or practical piety,
rather than its correlative and helpmeet. We
are reminded of words uttered by a dignitary of
the Church some few years ago, ' *We want happy
homes, not frequent services.*' But why not both ?
Shall we the better proclaim the precepts or
shepherd the lambs of God, by attending, with
sloven attitude and scanty shift of service, His
awful courts of praise ? Shall we take the

spikenard, due to Him, of the beauty that He
loves, and sell it for three hundred pence? Nay,
let us bestow all our goods to feed the poor;
but never rob the sacred treasuries of Him Who
said, 'Ye shall reverence My Sanctuary: I am
the Lord.' 'For this ought ye to have done, and
not to have left the other undone.' The great
motive assigned by Almighty God to the ancient
Pontiff for the reverent offering of the shadowy
sacrifices of the Law was this, '*that he die not.*'
What shall we say of the Oblation of the Lamb
that taketh away the sin of the world?

Yet by God's grace the picture has a brighter
side. And now that the Sacred Vestments of
the Church, in common with many other features
of Christian ceremonial, are by His goodness
so widely revived amongst us (*et attendat
studiose sacerdos ut signum sine significato non
ferat*) it may surely be supposed that many,
both clergy and laity, will be glad to hear their
story and learn their symbolism, from one of
the greatest and holiest Ritualists that ever
lived. The works of Durandus are always rare
and expensive, and are for the most part ancient

editions printed in Gothic letter, which with its blackness and frequent abbreviation is dazzling to the eye, and ill-adapted to a hurrying age.

The mediaeval mysticism of Durandus is not calculated to be acceptable to all. It has indeed been objected that he sets out with the deliberate intention of 'finding a meaning for everything.' But is not this a laudable intention? Has not the poet immortalised the spirit which

> ' Finds tongues in trees, books in the running brooks,
> Sermons in stones, and good in everything ' ?

I will add here, as Shakespeare adds,

> ' I would not change it.'

Such a mind at least compares favourably with the spirit—alas! all too prevalent even among the pious—which is content to take all things on trust ; which can look unmoved upon earthly and heavenly mysteries, and ask no question, feel no ' Divine curiosity,' as to their birth or message ; which can accept with grateful calm the immense heritage of the Faith, but never cares to scrutinise the golden coins that bear the superscription of the King. Unfortunate were that owner of a vast and beautiful estate, who should fulfil punctiliously the duties of the manor's lord, but never open a book in his library, nor muse before a picture on his gallery-walls, nor gaze with thoughtful wonder into the chalice of a single flower in his bright and wide parterres.

Quite true it is, that many a rite and instrument of worship has been born of utility and new-born of symbolism. The very word 'Use,' in liturgical phrase, testifies to this. Candles were burnt for their light, before ever men saw in them the emblem of the Light of Light. A maniple was employed for the meanest of uses, before ever it suggested the righteous '*portantes manipulos suos.*' But this is no argument against symbolism. It is rather a witness to its heavenly character. For if men devise a rite with a definitely symbolic purpose in the first instance, the charge of human invention will have an air of plausibility. But if, passing into it imperceptibly and naturally for its usefulness' sake, they realise afterwards that it is big with heavenly meaning, then all who behold it will be fain to cry out, '*A Domino factum est istud, et est mira-bile in oculis nostris.*'

All along the range of religious experience the principle holds good. It is often not until later life that men begin to trace an ordered design in the seemingly fortuitous happenings of earlier days. A common stone served Jacob for pillar at Luz, before ever he saw in it Beth-El, the House of God. It was a natural thing that One should ride into Jerusalem on an ass; so natural, that His disciples, paying little heed, 'understood not these things at the first; but when Jesus was glorified, then remembered they.' So the innumerable things and uses which were prest quite naturally into the service of the early Church were like obscure seeds cast into the ground; but it was holy ground, and sanctified the germs it nourished; and these sprang up in God's hour into beautiful flowers, brightening all the soil and sweetening all the air around the Tree of Life. '*For lo, the winter*' of obscurity '*is past, the rain*' of persecution '*is over and gone, and the flowers appear on the earth.*' But men perceived neither fragrance nor beauty, until the '*north wind awoke, and the south came, and blew upon My garden, that the spices thereof might flow out*'; and then they discerned that the thing was from the Lord.

Yet it is not true of our Bishop, that he is doggedly determined 'to find or invent a meaning for everything.' He is willing to leave much unexplained but by the primary principle of utility. 'It must carefully be noted,' he says in his general Proeme, 'that in the divine offices there be many customary rites which have, from their institution, respect neither unto a moral nor a mystical meaning. Of these, some are known to have arisen of necessity ; some of congruity ; some of the difference of the Old and New Testaments; some of convenience ; and some for the more honour and reverence of the offices themselves ; whence saith blessed Austin, "so many things are varied without number by the divers customs of divers places, that seldom or never can those causes be found out, which men followed in ordaining them."' His principle of finding symbolic reasons for long-established usages he justifies as follows : 'The

professors of the arts liberal, and of all arts
beside, if there be aught baldly and unadornedly
set forth therein, do give diligence to clothe,
support, and adorn it with causes and with
reasons. Painters moreover, and artificers and
handicraftsmen of what sort soever, do study in
all the divers branches of their works to render
and to have at hand probable reasons thereof.
So also it is unseemly for the magistrate to be
unknowing of this world's laws, and for the
advocate to know nought of that law, wherein
his daily work standeth.' For his right to a
certain freedom of exposition, and for his manner of using it, he makes this plea : ' As none are
prohibited (in the law) from using divers grounds
of exception and manners of defence, so neither
are they forbidden to use divers expositions in
the praise of God, provided only that the Faith
be kept whole.' And for aught blameworthy in
the book, which may have arisen from lack of
strength or wisdom or leisure, the Epilogue
which will be found inserted at the end of this
work makes ample and humble amends ; leaving
the most 'sober' critic surely fain to admire

the reverential devoutness, the prevailing Scrip-
tural tenour, the humility and dignity tempered
together, and above all things the sanctified
common-sense, of the work wherein the good
Bishop brings out of Holy Church's treasure
' things new and old.'

In the Notes I have aimed to keep a diversity
of readers in view. References to some authori-
ties are given for the sake of those who may
have a special interest in the subject; while
extracts are in most cases translated, and elemen-
tary details are briefly explained, for the benefit
of the less erudite. It has not been thought
necessary to give various readings in every
instance where they occur. In such cases I
have usually employed the variant which seemed
to me clearest, using as a basis the very satisfactory text of my own edition, a Venice folio
of 1491, printed in double columns by Ottaviano
Scotto, and unknown to Hain and Panzer.
This I have corrected by other editions in the
Bodleian where necessary.

The translation is as close as seems consis-
tent with English idiom. The quotations from

Holy Scripture, where the Vulgate permits, are in the words of the Authorised Version, except in the case of the Psalms, where they are given in the more familiar language of the Prayer-Book. The reader who desiderates that controversial treatment (as regards 'Roman claims' and so forth) which so often creeps into editions of works of this kind, will be under the necessity of supplying it for himself. 'Anglicanism' is not paraded, and 'Romanism' is not tiraded. 'Though I understand all mysteries, and have not charity, I am nothing.' Moreover, the book is a book on Ritual, and to that theme the notes are as far as possible confined. I may add that I have another and a more extensive Book of the *Rationale* in preparation, which I hope to produce should the present work prove acceptable.

It remains but to commend the latter to the all-wise and all-glorious Father of lights, in Whose Name and Whose honour alone our earthly service is offered, and without Whose acceptance and blessing no worship is holy, no sacrifice pure. '*Who hath seen Him, that he might tell us? and who can magnify Him as He* is ?   There are hid yet greater things than these be, for we have seen but a few of His works.   For the Lord hath made all things ; and to the godly hath He given wisdom.'

T. H. P.

LONDON :
Feast of St. Dunstan,
1899.

MEMOIR OF DURANDUS

WILLIAM DURANDUS was born at Puy-moisson, in the diocese of Béziers, in Languedoc. There is some uncertainty as to the date of his birth ; it was about the year 1230. Having studied canon law at the university of Bologna, he obtained his doctor's degree, and afterwards taught both at Bologna and Modena. By the year 1265 the fame of his skill and learning had reached the ear of Pope Clement IV., who appointed him Auditor of the Sacred Palace, Subdeacon and Chaplain to the Pope, and Canon of Beauvais and Narbonne. He rendered good service to Pope Gregory X., as his secretary, at the Council of Lyons in 1274. In 1277 he was made spiritual and temporal legate of the patrimony of S. Peter ; and in 1281 he became Vicar Spiritual, and in 1283 governor of the temporalities of the rebellious province

of Romagna, taking the lead of the war against
the rebels, and exerting himself to the utmost,
as Captain of the Papal forces, to secure the
Pope's authority. In pacifying this province
Durandus gave proof of great military and
administrative powers. In 1286 Pope Honorius
IV. made him Bishop of Mende, in Languedoc;
but he took possession of the see by proxy, and
so remained in Italy until 1291. During this
time he wrote much, and (it is thought) com-
pleted the *Rationale.* In 1295 Pope Boniface
VIII. offered him the Bishopric of Ravenna,
which he refused. About this time his strength
began to fail, and compelled him to resign office.
He retired to Rome, and closed a brilliant
career by death on All Saints' Day, 1296. His
monument is still to be seen in the Church of
Sta Maria sopra Minerva, with a lengthy inscription enumerating his writings and good
deeds. He was the survivor of sixteen Popes,
and the favourite of many.

    Some of the most famous works of Durandus
are the following :—*Speculum Judiciale* or *Juris*,
first published at Rome in folio, 1474; a practical treatise on civil and canon law, which
earned for its young author, at 34 years of age,
the names *Father of Practice*, and *Speculator.*

This work passed through thirty-eight editions between the years 1474 and 1678.

Repertorium Aureum or *Breviarium*, dedicated to Cardinal Matthaeus.

De Modo Concilii Generalis habendi.

Commentarius in Concilium Lugdunense.

The *Rationale Divinorum Officiorum*, of whose Third Book a translation is now presented to the reader, is an exhaustive treatise covering the whole range of Christian worship. It is divided into eight Books, to which the theme is apportioned as follows :—

The First Book treats of the Church and its parts.

The Second, of Church Ministers and Orders.

The Third, of the Vestments of Bishops, Priests, and Deacons.

The Fourth, of the Holy Mass and its parts.

The Fifth, of the Divine Offices of the Day and Night.

The Sixth, of the Sundays and Festivals of the year.

The Seventh, of Saints' Days.

The Eighth, of the Calendar.

It may be of interest to mention that the *Rationale* was the first book, from the pen of an

xxii The Sacred Vestments

uninspired writer, ever printed. The *editio princeps*, a magnificently beautiful book, and perhaps as rare as a book can be, was printed by Fust in 1459; being preceded only by the Psalters of 1457 and 1459. Besides this, Chalmers mentions thirteen editions in the fifteenth, and thirteen in the sixteenth century, all of which are very rare.[1]

The chief writers on Sacred Vestments with whose works Durandus gives evidence of familiarity, are as follows :—Josephus, Philo, S. Jerome (Letter to Fabiola, A.D. 396), Pope Celestine (A.D. 423–432), S. Isidore of Pelusium (*c.* A.D. 412), S. Gregory the Great (A.D. 590–604), S. Isidore of Seville (*c.* A.D. 560–636), Venerable Bede (*c.* A.D. 673–735), S. Germanus of Constantinople (*c.* A.D. 715), Rabanus Maurus (*c.* A.D. 822), Amalarius of Metz (*c.* A.D. 824), Walafrid Strabo (*c.* A.D. 842), Alcuin (*c.* A.D. 800), S. Ivo Carnotensis (*c.* A.D. 1100), Hugh of S. Victor (A.D. 1096–1140), Honorius of Autun (*c.* A.D. 1120), Pope Innocent III. (*c.* A.D. 1200).

---

[1] See Neale and Webb's *Symbolism,* Preface.

CONTENTS

CHAPTER I

PROEME

CHAPTER II

OF THE AMICE

CHAPTER X

OF THE TUNIC

CHAPTER X

OF THE DALMATIC

CHAPTER XII

OF THE GLOVES

CHAPTER XIII

OF THE MITRE

THE
SACRED VESTMENTS

CHAPTER I

PROEME

HERE beginneth the Book of the Vestments or Ornaments of the Church, as worn by Priests and Bishops, and other Ministers.

1. It behoveth not to wear the Sacred Vestments in the use of everyday.[1] Whereby we

[1] Vide 'Epist. Stephani R. P.' ap. Baron. ad An. 260.

mark, that even as we make change of vesture
according unto the letter, so we must do also
according unto the spirit. We may not enter
therefore into the Holy of Holies with garments
tainted by the use of common life ; but with a
pure conscience and with clean and holy raiment
must we handle the holy things of God. Wherefore Stephen,[1] Pope, did order that the Sacred
Vestments should not be used, save in the rites
of the Church, and in service meet for God ; as
saith Ezekiel in the forty-fourth chapter,[2] THEY
SHALL NOT SANCTIFY THE PEOPLE WITH
THEIR GARMENTS. One raiment therefore hath
Divine religion, for the Church's Offices ; and
another hath man for common use, to deliver

n. 6 ; Hieron. *in c.* 44 *Ezechiel* : 'Religio diuina alterum
habitum,' etc. Pelliccia thinks that anciently the Altar-dress
was identical in shape with the ordinary civilian dress, which
the clergy merely changed for a similar garb of better quality,
when about to celebrate (Lib. II. i. 8). The Church's Vestments certainly seem to have become the peculiar dress of the
clergy through growing obsolete among the laity. This is
worthy the consideration of those who condemn them as innova-
tions. — Bingham dates the distinction from the beginning of the
fourth century, on the ground that Constantine is said (Theod.
lib. ii. c. 27) to have given a rich gold-embroidered Vestment
to Macarius, Bishop of Jerusalem, to be worn by him when
celebrating Baptism.

   [1] Gratian, *Decretum*, 'De Consecratione,' Distinctio I. c.
xlii. ('Vestimenta'). Stephani Episc. Hilario (*Epist.* i. c. 5).
   [2] *v.* 19.

the lesson of good conversation unto all Christian folk : to the end that they, being washed from their former foulness, may be made new men in Christ. For at such a time the Priest doth doff the old man with his doings, and putteth on the new man, made in the image of God. By the Vestments, moreover, as worn only in sacred services, we do understand that not all holy things are to be unfolded unto the people. Note also that in the days of the Emperor Ludovic,[1] the son of Charlemagne, the Bishops and clergy laid aside their girdles wove with gold, and their exquisite garments and other trappings of this world.

2. Now the Sacred Vestments seem to have been taken from the Law of old. For the Lord gave commandment unto Moses that he should make for Aaron the High Priest and for his sons HOLY GARMENTS FOR GLORY AND FOR BEAUTY,[2] that being washed and clad in sacred vesture they might discharge their office in the sanctuary. For by the space of forty days the

---

[1] Louis I., called *le Débonnaire*, who reigned from 814 to 840 A.D. From the beginning of the sixth century right through the middle ages there were constant canons forbidding the gradually-increasing secularity and magnificence of the dress of the clergy ; notably at the Second Council of Nice (A.D. 787) the Council of Aix (A.D. 816), etc.

[2] Ex. xxviii. 2.

Lord did teach Moses to make pontifical and priestly vestments for His Priests and for the sons of Levi, yea, ornaments and robes of linen ; moreover, Miriam [1] wove and wrought them unto the use of the ministry of the Tabernacle of the Covenant. And so it is said in the forty-seventh chapter of Ecclesiasticus,[2] HE BEAUTI-FIED THEIR FEASTS. There be certain Vestments, on the other hand, which are taken from the Apostles : but both these and those do signify virtues, and express the ministry [3] of the Incarnation.

3. The Bishop, of a truth, when about to celebrate, doth put off his clothes of everyday, and arrayeth himself in garments pure and holy.

And first, he must put on the Sandals, that he may be mindful of the Incarnation of the Lord.

Secondly, he placeth upon himself the Amice, that he may restrain his motions and his thoughts, his lips and tongue, that he may have a clean heart, receiving a right spirit renewed within him.

Thirdly, the Albe, which reacheth to his

---

[1] Durandus says this either (i.) on the authority of some tradition, or (ii.) by analogy from the heathen practice recorded in 2 Kings xxiii. 7, ' the houses where the women wove hangings for the grove.'

[2] *v.* 10.   [3] V.l. *mysterium Incarnationis.*

feet; that he may have enduring purity in his flesh.

Fourthly, the Girdle, that he may rein in the impulse of desire.

In the fifth place, the Stole, for token of obedience.

In the sixth place, the Tunic, which is of blue, signifying heavenly conversation.

In the seventh place, he doth put on the Dalmatic, which is holy piety, and the mortifying of the flesh.

In the eighth place, the Gloves, that he refuse vainglory.

In the ninth place, the Ring, that he love his Bride, the Church, even as himself.

In the tenth place, the Chasuble, which is Charity.

In the eleventh place, the Napkin, that he wipe away with penance whereinsoever, through frailty or ignorance, he is a sinner.

In the twelfth place, he putteth on the Pall, to shew himself that he imitateth Christ, Who bare our sicknesses.[1]

In the thirteenth place, the Mitre, that he so live as to be worthy of receiving an eternal crown.

---

[1] S. Matth. viii. 17.

In the fourteenth place, he taketh the Staff, which is the authority of power and doctrine.

And after this he goeth upon carpets,[1] that he may learn to despise the earth, and to be in love with heavenly things. And with all these foregoing Vestments he is clad by his Ministers ; for the angels do minister unto him, that he may array himself in the garments of the Spirit : or because he is Vicegerent of Christ, unto Whom angels minister, and Whom all things serve.

The Bishop, then, looking toward the north —or toward the east, or the Altar, he may look, if it be more convenient—like a rescuer, a warrior about to fight with a long-standing foe, doth put on the Sacred Vestments as one accoutreth himself with arms, according to the Apostle, as I shall presently set forth.

4. First, the Sandals hath he for greaves of war, lest aught of the stain or dust of this world's affections cleave unto him. Secondly, with the Amice, as with an helm, he covereth his head. Thirdly, with the Albe, as with a breast-plate, he enveloppeth his whole body. Fourthly, he taketh the Girdle, to a bow, and

---

[1] *Tapeta* ; called in Old English 'tapets,' 'coverlets,' or 'pede cloaths' (Pugin).

the Undergirdle[1] to a quiver ; now the Undergirdle is that which hangeth down from the
Girdle, and wherewith the Bishop's stole is
fastened into the same. In the fifth place, with
the Stole he surroundeth his neck, as one that
brandisheth a spear in the face of his enemy.
In the sixth place, he taketh the Maniple, as
who wieldeth a club. Lastly, with the Chasuble
he covereth himself as it were with a shield ;
and with a Book he armeth his hand, as with a
sword. Of all the which I will speak singly in
different wise hereafter.

And so these are the accoutrements where-
with the Bishop or the Priest ought to arm
himself, willing to do battle against ghostly
wickedness. For thus saith the Apostle[2]:
THE WEAPONS OF OUR WARFARE ARE NOT
CARNAL; BUT MIGHTY TO THE PULLING
DOWN OF STRONGHOLDS. And in another
Epistle, that unto the Ephesians, in the sixth
cha, ter[3]:—PUT YE ON, saith he, THE ARMOUR
OF GOD, THAT YE MAY BE ABLE TO STAND
AGAINST THE WILES OF THE DEVIL. STAND
THEREFORE HAVING YOUR LOINS GIRT

---

[1] *Succinctorium*, a sash, called also *succingulum*, *succincta*,
and *praecinctorium*, formerly worn by all Bishops but now by
the Pope only. (Pugin.) See Ch. iv. of this work, note 4.

[2] 2 Cor. x. 4.   [3] vv. 13–17.

ABOUT WITH TRUTH, AND HAVING ON THE
BREASTPLATE OF RIGHTEOUSNESS, AND
YOUR FEET SHOD WITH THE PREPARATION
OF THE GOSPEL OF PEACE; ABOVE ALL
TAKING THE SHIELD OF FAITH, WHEREWITH
YE SHALL BE ABLE TO QUENCH ALL THE
FIERY DARTS OF THE WICKED: AND TAKE
THE HELMET OF SALVATION, AND THE
SWORD OF THE SPIRIT, WHICH IS THE WORD
OF GOD. Which armour is the foregoing
sevenfold priestly vesture, signifying the seven-
fold virtue of the Priest ; and representing more-
over the raiment of Christ wherewith He was
arrayed at the time of His Passion, as shall
be said anon.

5. Therefore the Bishop must take earnest
thought, and the Priest give careful heed, that
he bear not the sign without the thing signified :
that is, that he wear not the Vestment without
its virtue; lest perchance he be as a sepulcre,
whited without, BUT WITHIN FULL OF ALL
UNCLEANNESS.[1] For what Priest soever
adorneth himself with vestments, and putteth
not on good manners, the more worthy of
respect he seem unto men, so much the more
unworthy doth he become in the sight of God.

[1] S. Matth. xxiii. 27.

Wherefore the glory[1] of the Episcopate is not
approved by the splendour of garments, but by
brightness of souls : since those very adorn-
ments which did once delight the eyes of the
flesh did call the rather for those virtues which
were to be understood by their mean ; that
whatsoever those vestments with the gleam of
their gold, the sheen of their jewels, and the
variety of all kinds of broidery, did signify,
might in these latter days shine out in the
conduct and deed of the wearer. For even
amongst the ancients the form did win
reverence for its meaning, and in our own
days the experience of deeds is surer than the
riddle of symbols ; whereof, with other matters,
we read in the Pontifical, where it treateth of
the consecration of the Bishop.

6. So accoutred, then, for his conflict
AGAINST SPIRITUAL WICKEDNESS IN HIGH
PLACES, and for the allaying of the Judge's

---

[1] From this point to the end of the Section Durandus is
quoting, in a somewhat inverted manner, the words of the
Pontificale. They occur in a prayer offered by the Consecrator
(' De Consecratione Episcopi,' xx.). See also *Greg. Sacram.*,
Muratori, *Lit. Rom. Vet.* ii. 357. The passage had existed,
however, in the Gelasian form 100 years before S. Gregory
(Murat. i. 625). In connection with the Pontificale, it may be
interesting to state that Durandus himself wrote the MS. version
of it at the Vatican Library, No. 4744.

anger against His subjects, he proceedeth to the
Altar, and by the Confession doth renounce the
dominion of the devil, and accuseth himself;
and upon ordinary days the folk, as about to
pray for their champion, do prostrate themselves
upon the ground. When he uttereth the
Collects and other devotions, he doth fight as it
were with all his might against the devil.
When the Deacon before the Gospel upon Fast-
days foldeth back the Chasuble [1] over his
shoulder, he brandisheth as it were a sword
against the foe. When the Epistle is read, it
is the edicts of the Emperor that are being
proclaimed by the voice of the herald. The
chants are the trumpeters, the precentors ruling
the choir are the generals of the host marshal-
ing it unto battle, and as they lead the onset,
others come to their aid; and the strains of the
Sequence are the plaudits and the praise of
victory. When the Gospel is read, the foe is as
it were wounded with the sword, or scattered
forces after victory are gathered into line. The

---

[1] Durandus says elsewhere: 'The Deacon, being about to
read the Gospel, taketh off his Chasuble, and folding it in
seemly manner, placeth it upon his left shoulder, and fasteneth it
beneath his right arm, so that it shall fall from his left shoulder
unto his right side after the manner of a Stole; and keepeth it
in this wise bound upon him until the last Collect after the
Communion, when he putteth it on again as before.' (*Rat.* ii.
'De Diacono.')

Bishop, the while he preacheth, is the Emperor, lauding the conquerors ; the Oblations are the spoils, which the victors share ; and the strains of the Offertory are the triumph, due to the Emperor. The Pax[1] at the end is given unto the people, as a token of their quiet now that the foe is overthrown. And at the last the folk, after leave granted unto them in the *Ite missa est*,[2] depart again unto their own with gladness, for that victory and peace be won.

Wherefore the Priest, willing to celebrate Mass, must adorn himself with apparel which agreeth unto his order, and the beauty of his life must beseem his vesture's splendour.

7. Now in this matter it must be noted, that there be six Vestments[3] common unto both

---

[1] A small plate, generally of metal, was kissed by the Priest after the *Agnus Dei*, and then handed to the people, in token of the Kiss of Peace. But it is doubtful whether this was in common use so early as Durandus' time, as the first definite mention of it was in a Council held at Oxford in 1287, about the time of Durandus' appointment to the see of Mende. Doubtless he means the Kiss of Peace as given personally. See *Rat.* iv. 5:, 'De Pacis Osculo.'

[2] The concluding words of Holy Mass—'Go, it is done.'

[3] Durandus gives these as follows : the six powers common to both Bishops and Priests are to catechise, to baptise, to preach, to celebrate Mass, to bind, and to loose ; the nine peculiar to the Bishop, to ordain, to bless virgins, to consecrate Bishops, to lay on hands (confirm), to dedicate Churches, to degrade clerics, to call Synods, to consecrate the Chrism, and to consecrate vestments and vessels. (*Rat.* ii. 8, 'De Episcopo.')

Bishop and Priest, for that there be six matters wherein standeth such power as belongeth alike to both. Yet are there nine ornaments peculiar to the Bishop, because there are nine points wherein standeth such power as belongeth unto the Bishop alone. By this reckoning, then, of Vestments common and peculiar, are signified the functions common to both Bishop and Priest, and those peculiar to the former alone. Of such appointment, moreover, we read both in the Old and in the New Testament; for we are told that the High Priest, beside those garments which he had in common with the Priests, had also certain peculiar to himself. But in the Old Testament there were four common, and four peculiar, as shall be set forth in the chapter of the Vestments of the Law; and this, indeed, was demanded by mystic truth, for those Vestments were given unto carnal and worldly men. For unto the flesh the number four doth well agree, by reason of the four Humours; and unto the world, by reason of the four Elements. But these other are assigned unto them that are spiritual and perfect.

8. For the number six, which is a perfect number, in that it is made up of its own parts

added together, doth agree unto perfect things.
This is the reason that on the sixth day God
finished the heavens and the earth, AND ALL
THE HOST OF THEM; and furthermore, being
come in the fulness of time, in the sixth age, on
the sixth day, at the sixth hour, He redeemed
the sons of men. This number, I say, then, is
perfect, because it is made up exactly, if one
count it in the order of its parts. For when we
add one, two, and three, the number six is
fulfilled. For it is divided into three parts,
to wit, one-sixth, one-third, and a half, that
is one, two, and three. The number nine also
doth fit with spiritual things, because there are
nine orders of angels, which according to the
prophet are signified by nine kinds of precious
stones.[1]

9. Wherefore there are in all fifteen ornaments of the Bishop; and these by their number
do signify fifteen degrees of virtues, which the
Psalmist did mark out by as many Songs of
Degrees.[2] For the Priestly Vestments do mean
virtues, wherewith Priests ought to be adorned:
according unto that of the Prophet,[3] LET THY
PRIESTS BE CLOTHED WITH RIGHTEOUSNESS,

[1] Ezek. xxviii. 13.　　[2] Pss. cxx.–cxxxiv.
[3] Ps. cxxxii. 9.

AND LET THY SAINTS SING WITH JOYFUL-
NESS. And they are called *talares*, that is,
reaching unto the feet, because the foot is the
end of the body; by which it is set forth that to ·
begin a good work sufficeth not, save thou give
attention to fulfil it with perseverance even unto
the end; but of this more in the chapter of the
Tunic.

Thou seest, then, how that our Bishop putteth
on more than eight Vestments; whereas Aaron
had but eight, which have their counterparts
to-day; and this is to say that our RIGHTEOUS-
NESS MUST EXCEED THE RIGHTEOUSNESS OF
THE SCRIBES AND PHARISEES, if we would
ENTER INTO THE KINGDOM OF HEAVEN.[1]
On the other hand it may also be said that our
Bishop hath eight from head to feet, if we
except the ornaments of his feet and hands; to
wit, the Amice, the Albe, the Girdle, the Stole,
the two Tunics, the Chasuble, and the Pall.
For the vesting of the feet doth the rather
pertain unto our Pontiff than unto Aaron, since
unto the former it hath been said, GO YE AND
TEACH ALL NATIONS.[2]

Lastly, beside the foregoing Vestments
appointed unto Holy Orders and Ministers,

[1] S. Matth. v. 20.   [2] S. Matth. xxxviii. 19.

there remaineth yet another Vestment of linen,
called the Surplice, which those ought to wear
over their common dress, who have time that
they can give to any of the services of the Altar
and Sanctuary ; as shall be shown in the following chapter.

10. The Surplice, by reason that it is white,
doth point out the cleanness and purity of
chastity ; as it is written, LET THY GARMENTS
BE ALWAYS WHITE.[1]

11. And on account of its name it is a figure of
the mortification of the flesh, being called *superpellicium*, surplice, because of old it was wont to
be worn *super pellicias tunicas*, over tunics of
skin,[2] made of the hide of dead animals ; which
thing is observed in some churches to this day,
and figureth how Adam was clad in such skins
after his fall.

In the third place it denoteth innocence ;
and therefore is it often put on before all
other sacred Vestments,[3] because they that are
appointed unto the ministry of Divine worship

[1] Eccles. ix. 8.

[2] Fur robes were worn of old in choir, as a protection
against cold, especially in northern countries such as England ;
and hence the word *superpellicium* is found often in old English
monuments.

[3] ' Priests about to celebrate Mass shall not be without a
Surplice (*vestis camisialis*) under their Albes ' (Council of

ought to count innocency of life the first of all acts of virtue; according unto that of the Psalmist,[1] THE INNOCENT AND JUST HAVE CLOVEN UNTO ME.

12. In the fourth place, by its fulness,[2] it doth meetly express charity, wherefore it is put on over profane and common garments, to mark that CHARITY COVERETH THE MULTITUDE OF SINS.[3] Lastly by its shape—for it is wrought in the form of a cross—it representeth our Lord's Passion, and that they who wear it ought to crucify the flesh, with its vices and lusts.[4]

13. In some places surplices are made of linen √ chrisoms,[5] which are put upon infants baptised;

Cologne, A.D. 1260). So also the Canons of the Church of Liège, A.D. 1287. Durandus is one of the earliest writers who mention the Surplice, though it had been in use long before his time.

[1] Ps. xxv. 21 (Vulgate).

[2] *Pace* those who loudly boast the special antiquity of the Surplice, it seems certain that it was a modification of the Albe, made fuller and ampler, to enable it to be worn over the fur garments of which Durandus speaks; and that the very *rationale* of its existence was to be *full*, unlike its modern Anglican development. As late as 1339 a Constitution of Benedict XII. orders that Surplices be ' large and ample.' We hear much of the ' beauty ' and ' grace ' of the close-fitting cathedral surplice. It is as ugly and ungainly as the girded Albe, its prototype, is dignified and beautiful.

[3] 1 S. Pet. iv. 8.   [4] Gal. v. 24.

[5] White cloths which the Priest put on the newly-baptised, with the words ' Accipe uestem candidam, quam immaculatam

after the example of Moses, who of the purple
and fine linen and other things offered of the
people in the Tabernacle, did make garments
for Aaron and his sons to put on, when they
ministered in the sanctuary.[1]

There is moreover another Vestment, which
√ is called the Pluvial[2] or Cope. This is believed
to have been borrowed from the Tunic of the
Law; wherefore, as that was ornamented with
little bells, so is this embroidered with fringes,
which are labours and cares of this world.[3] An
hood[4] also it hath, which is heavenly delight;
and it is long, reaching unto the feet, which
signifieth perseverance to the end. In the forepart it is open, to denote that unto holy livers
eternal life is open, and that their own life ought
to be an open ensample unto others. And

perferas ante tribunal D. N. J. C., ut habeas uitam aeternam.'
It was anciently a long robe, like a hooded Albe.

[1] Ex. xxxix. I.

[2] Because it was originally a cloak to serve against rain. It
is now principally an Episcopal Vestment, but is worn by Priests
in processions, in Choir, and at solemn functions. . It is supposed by many to have been the original of the Chasuble.

[3] In the sacristy of Aix-la-Chapelle Cathedral is still preserved a Cope, said to have been worn by Leo III., having
small silver bells on its lower edge.

[4] The modern ornamental hood on the Cope, dating from
the fourteenth century, is a survival of a real hood, which could
be put over the head.

C

further, by the Cope we understand the glorious immortality of our bodies : wherefore we wear it not, save on the greater Feasts; having respect unto the Resurrection to come, when the elect, laying aside the flesh, shall receive two garments, rest of soul and body's glory. This Vestment also, as well beseemeth, is ample within, nor is joined but by one necessary fastening [1] ; because the body, rendered spiritual, shall in that day by no narrowness cloke up the soul. And it is provided with a fringe, because nought shall then be lacking unto our own perfection, but that which WE NOW KNOW IN PART WE SHALL THEN KNOW EVEN AS ALSO WE ARE KNOWN.[2]

14. But certain heretics [3] do vainly talk, affirming that this can nowhere be found in the New Testament, that Christ or His disciples did put on the Vestments foregoing ; rashly censuring us for that we adorn ourselves with such things, when as Saint John saith,[4] THE LORD

[1] The Morse, a clasp which fastened the Cope before the breast ; it was, and is, often richly jewelled.

[2] 1 Cor. xiii. 12.

[3] Here and there in Durandus and his contemporaries, we come across passages which would seem to show that the Protestant spirit is older than it is popularly supposed to be.

[4] S. John xiii. 4.

RISING FROM 'SUPPER LAID ASIDE HIS
GARMENTS, and did after take unto Him none
save only His own [1]; yet that we do put on many
other than those we ordinarily wear, in the Mass,
wherein we follow that very Feast; whereas the
Lord hath bidden us beware of them that love
to walk in long garments, saying, BEWARE OF
THE SCRIBES, WHICH DESIRE TO WALK IN
LONG ROBES.[2] They say, too, that we do this
to appear more righteous and better than the
people, in despite of that which is said, YE ARE
THEY WHICH JUSTIFY YOURSELVES BEFORE
MEN; BUT GOD KNOWETH YOUR HEARTS:
FOR THAT WHICH IS HIGHLY ESTEEMED
AMONG MEN IS ABOMINATION IN THE SIGHT
OF GOD.[3]

But their error is most plainly confounded
by that which goeth before. For in Ezechiel [4]
also we read, in the forty-second and forty-fourth
chapters, WHEN THEY SHALL ENTER INTO
MY SANCTUARY, AND SHALL COME NEAR TO
MY TABLE, TO MINISTER UNTO ME, AND TO
KEEP MY CHARGE, THEY SHALL BE CLOTHED
WITH LINEN GARMENTS, AND NO WOOL
SHALL COME UPON THEM, AND WHEN THEY

---

[1] S. John xiii. 12.   [2] S. Luke xx. 46.   [3] *Ibid.* xvi. 15.
[4] Ezek. xlii. 14, and xliv. 16, 17, 19.

GO FORTH INTO THE UTTER COURT TO THE
PEOPLE, THEY SHALL PUT OFF THEIR GAR-
MENTS WHEREIN THEY MINISTERED : AND
THEY SHALL NOT SANCTIFY THE PEOPLE
WITH THEIR GARMENTS.

15. Mark, furthermore, that the doorkeepers,
readers, exorcists and acolyths [1] wear white
vestments, that is to say, Surplice, Amice, Albe,
and Girdle, that in the cleanness of their purity
they may imitate the angels which are the
ministers of God, and may company with them
as it were in the white robe of a body made
spiritual and glorious. Therefore do they wear
vestments of linen, rather than any other ; for
as flax is not brought unto whiteness save by
much toil, so it needeth to pass through many
tribulations, if thou wouldst win to the glory of
the Kingdom.

16. By the Council of Mayence [2] it hath been
appointed that the Bishop, at his ordination,
should receive a Stole, a Staff, and a Ring ; the

[1] Minor Orders. There are seven of these as given by
Durandus : Cantor, Psalmist, Ostiarius (or Porter), Lector (or
Reader), Exorcist, Acolyth, and Subdeacon.

[2] It was the Fourth Council of Toledo (A.D. 633, c. 28)
that made this enactment. It is called the 'Instrumentorum
Traditio,' and was looked upon in the seventh century as an
integral part of the outward sign of the bestowal of Order.
(See Martene, *De Rit. Ant.* I. viii. 9, § 16.)

Priest, a Stole and a Chasuble; the Deacon, a Stole and a Dalmatic,[1] and the Subdeacon a Paten and Chalice; which all, if they be degraded, must render up. And by the Council of Toledo[2] it hath been ruled that the Deacon shall wear 'the white Vestment'—that is, the Dalmatic—only at the time of the Offering, wherein he readeth the Gospel.

17. Also it is to be observed, that the Vestments of the Priest of the Gospel have certain meanings in regard of the Head, which is Christ, and certain in regard of the members, albeit both Head and Members be called by the Priestly name; as saith the Psalmist[3] unto the Head, THOU ART A PRIEST FOR EVER AFTER THE ORDER OF MELCHISEDECH; and to the members saith the Apostle,[4] YE ARE A CHOSEN

[1] The words of the Council are 'Diaconus, omnium et albam.' But here, as in the next sentence, Durandus interprets alba as Dalmatic.

[2] Gratian, Decr. I. Dist. xciii. ('Diaconus alba tantum tempore Oblationis et lectionis utatur.') The Fourth Council of Carthage, at the end of the fourth century, enacted this (can. 41). And it seems likely that the true Albe was meant. The canon probably intended that Bishops and Priests should wear this Vestment ordinarily, but Deacons only at the time named. There seems to have been a growing tendency on the part of Deacons to assume the dress of the higher orders. It is noteworthy that this is the first mention of the word 'Alba' technically as denoting a Christian Vestment.

[3] Ps. cx. 4.   [4] 1 S. Pet. ii. 9.

GENERATION, A ROYAL PRIESTHOOD. Therefore their mystic meanings are to be expounded, first, as touching that which agreeth unto the members, secondly as touching that which agreeth unto the Head, which is Christ. And after this manner I shall distinguish in every chapter.

18. The six Vestments, then, which be common to both Bishop and Priest, are these :—

The Amice.	The Stole.
The Albe.	The Maniple.
The Zone, or Girdle.	The Chasuble.

And the nine which be peculiar to the Bishop are these :—

The Buskins.	The Dalmatic.
The Sandals.	The Gloves.
The Undergirdle.	The Mitre.
The Tunic.	The Ring.

The Pastoral Staff.

Of all the which in turn we will go on to speak, as also of the Napkin, the Pall, and of the Colours which the Church useth in her Vestments ; and also of the Vestments of the Law, or of the Old Testament.

CHAPTER II

OF THE AMICE.

1. Of the Amice, its use and meaning.—2. Of the Amice as wrapt around neck and breast.—3. Of the Amice as touching the Lord's Incarnation.

1. FIRST I must speak of the six Vestments common to both Bishop and Priest, according to the foregoing.

The Priest or Bishop who is about to celebrate, having washed his hands, taketh the Amice, and covereth his head [1] with it ; and this he hath in the stead of the Ephod or Super humeral, or of the Breastplate of Judgment [2] ;

---

[1] The Amice (*amictus*), which is now put round the neck, is thought by some to have been originally a head-vestment. There was an old French custom of wearing it on the head at certain times of the year and in certain parts of Mass, and letting it fall down over the shoulders at others to signify reverence. To this day the Priest, in vesting for Mass, rests it on his head before letting it down over his shoulders. The strings which are fastened to its corners are crossed over the breast, passed behind the back, and tied before the breast. It is nowhere mentioned as a Vestment until the ninth century.

[2] Ex. xxxviii. 30. See the last Chapter of this work, § 12.

nay, even now it may be called the Super-
humeral. This signifieth salvation, which is
granted through faith ; whereof also the Apostle
speaketh, saying unto the Ephesians,[1] PUT ON
THE HELMET OF SALVATION. It figureth also
chastity of heart and body, because it goeth
round his reins and breast, and covereth them ;
and though it be put on beneath all other
sacred Vestments,[2] yet it is supreme over all,
for that chastity ought both to dwell within the
heart, and in practice to shine out abroad.
Wherefore it is drawn tight over the reins, for
there desire doth hold his chief sway. Moreover, by the Amice is signified that a man
should be strong in good works, for it spreadeth
over the shoulders every way :[3] and it is the
shoulders that be strong unto the carrying-out
of labour, even as the patriarch Jacob saith, HE
BOWED HIS SHOULDER TO BEAR, AND BECAME
A SERVANT UNTO TRIBUTE.[4]

There be two strings wherewith the Amice
is tied across the breast ; these are the intention

---

[1] Eph. vi. 17.

[2] Martene tells us that the Amice was formerly put on over
the Albe.

[3] So Hugh of S. Victor, L. i. *Erudit. Theolog.* c. 45, and
Innocent III., Lib. I. *De Myst. Missae*, c. 50.

[4] Gen. xlix. 15.

wherewith, and the end whereunto, our works
must be informed, that they be not done
in the leaven of malice and wickedness,
but in the unleavened bread of sincerity and
truth.[1] Thus ought not the Priest to live
in idleness, but to labour in good works, according to that of the Apostle unto Timothy,[2]
LABOUR AS A GOOD SOLDIER OF JESUS CHRIST.
In certain places a praiseworthy custom holdeth,
that a white shift of linen, or a surplice, should
be put on over the common dress before the
Amice[3]; whereby faith is understood, which
ought to be had before all things. Again, the
Amice goeth round the mouth of the Chasuble ;
but of this I will treat in the chapter of the
Chasuble.

   2. The Amice is drawn tightly round the neck :
and by this is symbolised the subjection of the
voice, for the neck, wherein is the voice,[4] doth
express the act of speaking ; it is therefore held
bound, as it were, lest falsehood pass unto the
tongue therefrom. Yet over the breast and
throat it is drawn but loosely, as shall be
expounded in the chapter of the Girdle. With

---

[1] 1 Cor. v. 8.   [2] 2 Tim. ii. 3.   [3] See Proeme, p. 15, *n.* 3.
[4] So Fortunatus, Archbishop of Trèves, L. ii. *De Divin.*
Offic. c. 17.

the Amice also we cover the head, lest, if we
cast the eyes freely every way, we should ponder
unlawful things. And the breast and heart are
covered with it, for the mind of the Priest ought
to be all intent on those things which lie upon
him ; nor may he in that hour relax his heart
unto vanities, or to the unrestrained meditation
of any worldly thing.

3. Further, as touching that which agreeth
unto the Head, even Christ, the Amice, which
overshadoweth the Priest's head, doth represent
that which is described in the Apocalypse,[1] AND
I SAW A MIGHTY ANGEL COME DOWN FROM
HEAVEN, CLOTHED WITH A CLOUD ; and in
Esaias,[2] BEHOLD, THE LORD RIDETH UPON A
SWIFT CLOUD. And the world's Saviour, the
Son of God, the Angel of Great Counsel, coming
to save the world, was veiled as with a cloud,
when He hid away His Godhead in Flesh. For
THE HEAD OF EVERY MAN IS CHRIST ; AND
THE HEAD OF CHRIST IS GOD.[3]

The Priest's Amice, then, doth symbolise
this hiding in Flesh ; but it is more particularly
set forth by that Veil [4] which the Holy Father

[1] Rev. x. 1.
[2] Is. xix. 1.   Vulg. says *levem*, not *candidam*, as Durandus.
[3] 1 Cor. xi. 3.
[4] The Fanon or Orale, which (as Georgius tells us, Lib. I.

draweth over his head, and of which I will speak
in the chapter of the Undergirdle.   And it is
a comely thought that this very thing, which is
typified by the shoes of the feet, is also ex-
pressed by the veiling of the head—namely, the
lying-hid of the Godhead in Flesh, and Its
revelation through it.   For when HE WAS
KNOWN IN JEWRY, AND HIS NAME WAS GREAT
IN ISRAEL[1]; then OVER EDOM DID HE CAST
OUT HIS SHOE,[2] and HIS RIGHTEOUSNESS DID
HE OPENLY SHOW IN THE SIGHT OF THE
HEATHEN.[3]

The Amice doth also represent the fold
wherewith the Jews veiled the Face of Christ,
saying in the twenty-sixth chapter of Matthew,[4]
PROPHESY UNTO US, THOU CHRIST, WHO IS
HE THAT SMOTE THEE?

c. xviii.) is a striped veil of four colours, put on by the Pope
after the Girdle, and turned back over the head.   After the
Chasuble is put on, it is brought down over the shoulders and
breast.   Durandus gives a similar description of it in the chapter
referred to.

[1] Ps. lxxvi. 1.   [2] Ibid. lx. 8.   [3] Ibid. xcvii 2.
[4] S. Matth. xxvi. 68.

CHAPTER III·

OF THE ALBE

1. Of the Albe and its meaning. —2. Of byssus.—3, 4. Of the making and form of the Albe in the Old and New Testaments.—5. Of the sleeves, and of the length of the Albe. 6. Of the Albe as touching Christ.

1. AFTER the Amice the Priest putteth on him a shift called the Albe ; and this, being exactly fitted to all the limbs of the body, doth show that there must be nought of excess or looseness in the life of the Priest, or in his members. By its whiteness it doth represent purity ; for it is written, LET THY GARMENTS BE ALWAYS WHITE ;[1] and it is made of byssus, or fine linen, for it is written that FINE LINEN IS THE RIGHTEOUSNESS OF SAINTS.[2]

2. Now byssus is Egyptian linen. And even as linen, or byssus, doth win by cunning, being beaten with many blows, that whiteness which by nature it hath not ; so also man's flesh,

---

[1] Eccles. ix. 8.   [2] Rev. xix. 8.

being lashed with many stripes [1] in the exercise
of good works, hath by grace that pureness
allotted unto it which by nature it cannot have.
The Priest therefore, according unto the
Apostle,[2] must BUFFET HIS BODY, AND BRING
IT INTO SUBJECTION, LEST THAT BY ANY
MEANS, WHEN HE HATH PREACHED TO
OTHERS, HIMSELF SHOULD BE A CASTAWAY.

3. The Albe hath also an hood,[3] the pro-
fession of chastity ; and a lappet, signifying the
priestly tongue, which bindeth the froward, and
looseth the penitent. Again, this Vestment,
which in the ancient priesthood was called a
linen coat, and in Greek ποδήρης, or the garment which reacheth unto the feet, is said of
old to have been closely-fitting, which pointeth
unto the Jews' SPIRIT OF BONDAGE TO FEAR.[4]
But in the new Priesthood it is ample, according

---

[1] 'Comme elle [l'Aube] se blanchit dans l'eau, et avec des
grands soins, cela nous marque que notre pureté nous vient de
l'eau spirituelle, des larmes qu'une sainte pénitence nous fait
couler de nos yeux' (*Explication du Breviaire et du Missel*,
par M. Raymond Bonal, prêtre de Lyons, 1679). See Pugin
under 'Albe.'

[2] 1 Cor. ix. 27.

[3] So also had the Chasuble, which S. Isidore describes as
'casula, uestis cucullata'; and the Colobium, which was probably the prototype of the Tunicle ; also the Cope, with most
Vestments originally designed for outdoor use.

[4] *Cf.* Rom. viii. 15.

to the spirit of adoption, in that LIBERTY
WHEREWITH CHRIST HATH MADE US FREE.[1]
It hath also golden broidery and devices[2] for
ornament wrought with varied work in divers
parts, which hinteth of that which the Prophet
saith in the Psalms,[3] UPON THY RIGHT HAND
DID STAND THE QUEEN IN A VESTURE OF
GOLD, WROUGHT ABOUT WITH DIVERS
COLOURS.

4. The Albe is also drawn tight with a
girdle, and this meaneth the strangling of all
carnal pleasure, as the Lord saith, LET YOUR
LOINS BE GIRT.[4]

5. And the sleeves of the Albe, as also of
the Tunicle, ought to be tight enow, not too
loose, lest they slip away and leave the arms
bare ; and having apparels at the edges, repre-

---

[1] Gal. v. 1.

[2] These 'Apparels,' as they are called, which the Albe has
in common with its correlative the Amice, are very ancient.
They formed part of the Vestment even in the old time when it
was a civilian's dress, and were then usually purple (Vopisc.
in Aureliano, c. 48). They were, and still are, sewn in round
the sleeve-edges and the bottom of the skirts ; were very various
in their decoration, and usually angular in shape ; and were
beginning to be specially ornate and extensive at the time when
Durandus wrote.

[3] Ps. xlv. 10. All this is closely borrowed from Innocent
III.

[4] S. Luke xii. 35.

senting the golden bracelets which by a miracle
did enclose in seemly wise the bare arms of
Saint Martin [1] while he celebrated Mass. By the
Albe also, which covereth the body from above
downwards, is typified that hope which cometh
unto the Church from above through grace,
and through her own merits below. Of this
the Apostle saith,[2] WE ARE SAVED BY HOPE.
And in that it reacheth unto the feet, it pointeth

---

[1] Durandus thus tells the story elsewhere:—'When he
[S. Martin] was Archbishop of Tours, there came a poor and
needy man unto him, begging for a coat. The Saint granted
the hest, and sent his steward to buy one. The latter went
into the market, and returned after a long while with a cheap
cloak, which one might well have called a *paenula* (mantle) for
it was *paene nulla*, next to nothing ! The holy man bade show
it to him ; now it was very short, reaching but unto the knee,
and the sleeves to the elbow ; wherefore he took off his own
cloak and gave it to the poor man, and himself put on this
pauper garment. Not long after this, the Saint made him ready
to say Mass ; when, as he stood at the Altar and at the Preface,
as is the wont of priests, uplifted his hands unto the Lord, the
loose sleeves of the mantle aforesaid slipped back—for his arms
were not much covered with flesh—and so left his arms bare.
Whereupon there came miraculous bracelets of gold, and
covered his bare arms in seemly manner, and a ball of fire
appeared above his head ; whereby it was made plain that the
Holy Spirit had come down upon him to his comfort, as upon
the Apostles at Pentecost. And hence he is not undeservedly
called Peer of the Apostles, with whom we place him on a par
in the Offices of the Church.' (*Rat.* L. vii. ' De beato Martino.')
His day (Nov. 11) is a double in the Roman Calendar.

[2] Rom. viii. 24.

to perseverance, as was mentioned near the
end of the Proeme of this Book.

6. But as touching that which agreeth unto
Christ, Which is the Head ; the Albe being a
linen vestment, and widely differing from the
clokes made of the skins of dead animals,
wherewith Adam was clad after his fall, doth
picture that newness of life which Christ both
had and taught, and doth give in Baptism unto
us. And concerning this the Apostle [1] saith,
PUT OFF THE OLD MAN WITH HIS DEEDS,
AND PUT ON THE NEW MAN, WHICH IS
CREATED AFTER GOD. For in the Transfigura-
tion HIS FACE DID SHINE AS THE SUN, AND HIS
RAIMENT WAS WHITE AS SNOW [2]; nay, the
garments of Christ were ever white and clean,
forasmuch as HE DID NO SIN, NEITHER WAS
GUILE FOUND IN HIS MOUTH. [3]

This Vestment representeth also the white
robe,[4] which Herod put on Christ to mock Him.

[1] Col. iii. 9, 10, and Eph. iv. 24.
[2] S. Matth. xvii. 2, and S. Mark ix. 3.
[3] 1 S. Pet. ii. 22.   [4] S. Luke xxiii. 11.

CHAPTER IV

OF THE ZONE, OR GIRDLE

1. Of the Girdle and its meaning.—2. Of the Undergirdle. 3, 4. Of Continence and Abstinence, as set forth by them both.—5. Of the Girdle, and the parts it goeth round.—6. Of its meanings as touching Christ.

1. Now the Albe must be girded around the loins of the Priest or Bishop with a Zone or Girdle, called in the Law and by the Greeks *balteus*,[1] lest it flow down and hinder his steps; that no motives may provoke him to relax his chasteness, whereof the Albe is a type. For the Girdle doth signify continence, as it is written,

[1] See Ex. xxviii. 4, Vulg. 'Balteus' is allied with our word 'belt.' The Girdle, like most other Vestments, has dwindled in size. In early times it was larger, and more ornate; as Bishop Riculfus in his will bequeaths 'five girdles, one adorned with gold and precious stones, and four more with gold.' Girdles were used by the ancients as purses; hence their old Greek name καταθεσλαι—repositories. See Pelliccia, Lib. I. c. viii. 2. S. Chrysostom (*Hom. in Psal.* 48; vol. v. 521) inveighs against luxury in dress, and especially against golden girdles. Which secular sumptuousness the Girdle preserved, long after it had become a Vestment of the Church.

D

LET YOUR LOINS BE GIRDED ABOUT, AND YOUR
LAMPS BURNING IN YOUR HANDS [1]; for that in
the loins lust reigneth, as the Lord sheweth,
speaking of the devil, HIS STRENGTH IS IN HIS
LOINS, AND HIS FORCE IS IN THE NAVEL OF
HIS BELLY.[2]

2. On the left side of the Bishop there
hangeth down from the Girdle a two-fold
Undergirdle,[3] because there be two things
whereby Chastity is made strong, and without
which it is hardly preserved, to wit, Prayer and
Fasting.   Thus the Lord saith, THIS KIND
GOETH NOT OUT, BUT BY PRAYER AND
FASTING.[4]

3. With Continence, therefore, ought the
loins to be girded, and under-girded with
Abstinence; wherefore the Apostle,[5] STAND
HAVING YOUR LOINS GIRT ABOUT WITH

---

[1] S. Luke xii. 35.

[2] Job xl. 16.   It is also good to think of the Girdle as a
type of continence because it is the means of keeping the skirts
out of the mire.

[3] 'In the Caeremoniale S.R.E. it is ordered that the Pope
be vested with a Girdle having a Succinctorium, or sash, hanging down on the left side. . . . Pope Boniface was found in
his tomb with a rochet girt about with a sash of leather, covered
with red silk, like to a belt, with four cords of red silk hanging
in front, which fastened the Girdle.' (Pugin, *Gloss. Ecc. Orn.*,
under 'Girdle.')   See Proeme, p. 7, *n.* 1.

[4] S. Matth. xvii. 21.   [5] Eph. vi. 14.

TRUTH. But the Undergirdle, which is called otherwise *Perizona* or *Succingulum*, was not found among the Vestments of the Law. For though the Priests of the Law, being girded, must not come at their wives in the time of sacrifice, yet at other times they were free in this matter. But nowadays one girdle is added, for the ministers of to-day must needs have continence, and therefore they must be not only girded, but also under-girded.

4. Wherefore the Undergirdle is twofold, ✓ to denote a two-fold chastity : namely, of the mind, as the Girdle, and of the body, as the Undergirdle signifieth. And this latter hangeth, as I have said, from the left side ; for as the right is mightier than the left, so is chastity of mind more potent than chastity of body. Wherefore Saint Gregory saith, 'We gird our loins, when we restrain the lust of the flesh through continence.'

5. The Girdle doth also fitly designate temperance. (Of the Undergirdle I have spoken also in the Proeme[1] of this Book.) And mark that (as hath been already said) the breast and throat are but loosely held bound by the Amice, because their motions are not

[1] Sec. 4.

under our power. Elias did sooner shut up heaven when he prayed that it might not rain, than his own wrath, when he desired vengeance for the death of the prophets.[1] The tongue, too, dwelleth in moisture and dampness, and is made easily to slip, even as the Prince of the Apostles did at the word of a damsel deny his Master. But by the Girdle the reins are bound strongly and tightly, that we may buffet the body and bring it into servitude, and may bridle the motions of lust.[2]

6. As touching that which agreeth unto the Head, even Christ, the priestly Girdle is a figure of that whereof the Apostle John[3] speaketh: AND I TURNED, AND SAW ONE LIKE UNTO THE SON OF MAN, GIRT ABOUT THE PAPS WITH A GOLDEN GIRDLE. By a 'golden girdle' is intended the perfect love of Christ, called by the Apostle[4] the LOVE OF CHRIST WHICH PASSETH KNOWLEDGE, burning within the heart, and shining forth in works. And its Undergirdle doth represent that which Esaias[5] did prophesy, speaking of Christ, AND RIGHTEOUSNESS SHALL BE THE GIRDLE OF HIS

---

[1] Those mentioned in 1 Kings xviii. 13 as slain by Jezebel.
[2] 1 Cor. ix. 27.   [3] Rev. i. 12, 13.
[4] Eph. iii. 19.   [5] Is. xi. 5.

LOINS, AND FAITHFULNESS THE GIRDLE OF
HIS REINS. For again, THE RIGHTEOUS LORD
LOVETH RIGHTEOUSNESS : HIS COUNTENANCE
WILL BEHOLD THE THING THAT IS JUST.[1]
And, THE LORD IS RIGHTEOUS IN ALL HIS
WORKS.[2] The two ends of it are the two
natural precepts of the righteousness which
Christ wrought and taught, to wit, ' Do not
unto others as ye would not have them do unto
you, but as ye would that men should do unto
you, do ye also unto them.'[3] It doth therefore represent Righteousness, having two arms
joined tightly together, that is, to refuse evil
and to do good.

The Girdle signifieth also the scourge, with
which Pilate did scourge Jesus.[4]

[1] Ps. xi. 8.   [2] *Ibid.* cxlv. 17.
[3] Expanded from S. Luke vi. 31.   [4] S. John xix. 1.

CHAPTER V

OF THE STOLE

1. Of the Stole and its meaning.—2. Why the Stole reacheth unto the knees, and is girded.—3. Why the Stole goeth over the shoulders, and maketh a cross upon the breast.—4. Of the Stole in the Priest, and in the Deacon.—5. Why the Stole is girt round at the loins.—6. Why the Stole is called Orarium ; and of the ancient Stole.—7. Of the Stole as touching Christ.—8. Of certain who may not wear the Stole.

1. AFTER the Girdle the Priest doth put upon his neck the Orarium,[1] or Stole, which is a type

---

[1] Thought to be derived from *ora*, a border. It has been thought that the Orarium was in some way distinct from the Stole. In the Life of S. Livinus we are told that the Saint was given by S. Augustine of Canterbury, on the day of his ordination, a *Stole with an Orarium*, enriched with jewels. It may be that the word was formerly applied to the ornamental *border* of a large Vestment now obsolete, which was called *Stola*; and that this Vestment gradually dwindled in size, until nothing was left of it but the said border, which survived under the interchangeable names of Orarium and Stole. For the old classical word στολή, *stola*, as is well known, meant a feminine garment with sleeves, covering the whole person : Hor. *Sat.* Lib. I. ii. 99, 'Ad talos Stola demissa.' And Pugin tells us that in the plates of Bosio's *Roma Sotterranea* the Stole is represented in its ancient form, with the present Stole as a stripe or orfrey. Durandus himself, in § 6, implies that the Stole was once larger than it was in his time. Others, however, condemn this view,

of the light yoke of Christ, or of the yoke of
His precepts, to show that he hath taken the
Lord's yoke upon him. This he doth kiss in
putting it on and off, to mark the consent and
desire wherewith he submitteth himself to that
yoke. And it falleth down from the neck
before, adorning both the right side and the
left ; for BY THE ARMOUR OF RIGHTEOUSNESS
ON THE RIGHT HAND AND ON THE LEFT,[1]
that is, in weal and woe, the Priest ought to be
armed, that he be neither broken by misfortunes
nor lifted up by well-being. Wherefore when
the Priest receiveth the Stole in Holy Order,
the Bishop saith[2] unto him, 'Receive the yoke
of God, FOR HIS YOKE IS SWEET, AND HIS
BURTHEN IS LIGHT ;' that is, sweet in well-
being, and in misfortune light.

2. The Stole reacheth down to the knees,
which are bent by us as showing that we must
be humble and gentle of heart. It signifieth
also patience, whereof it is written, YE HAVE

and connect Ornrium with *os*, the face, regarding the Stole as
having originated from a kerchief or napkin. The etymology of
the word is further touched on in note 2, p. 43.

[1] 2 Cor. vi. 7.

[2] This the Pontifical directs the Bishop to say; while he
arranges the Stole before the Priest's breast in the form of a
cross. *Pontificale Rom.* Pars I. Titul. XII. § viii.

NEED OF PATIENCE, THAT YE MIGHT RECEIVE
THE PROMISE[1]; and again, IN YOUR PATIENCE
YE SHALL POSSESS YOUR SOULS.[2] Hence it
ariseth that the Stole is tied in certain knots on
the right and on the left, with the Zone or
Girdle, for virtue doth company with virtue and
succoureth it, lest by some impulse temptation
be stirred up; which showeth also that both in
things good and in things evil the yoke of
Christ ought patiently to be borne, in the bond
of charity.[3]   But unto the foregoing some
Bishops do add these words, 'May the Lord
clothe thee with the Stole of innocence';[4] and
this hath respect unto the Stole in its olden
shape,[5] which was typical of innocence.

3. Again, the Stole is crossed[6] over from the
√ left shoulder of the Priest unto his right side,
while he is ordained, for obedience, taking its
beginning from the active life through the love

[1] Heb. x. 36.
[2] S. Luke xxi. 19.   The A.V., 'possess ye,' represents the
other reading, κτησασθε.   But κτησεσθε (Vulg. *possidebitis*, and
R.V. 'ye shall win') is preferable both as regards authority and
meaning.
[3] See Col. iii. 14.
[4] More correctly, the Bishop says these words while unfold-
ing the Chasuble which the Priest wears folded over his shoulder.
Pontificale, P. I. Tit. XII. § xxviii.
[5] See p. 45, *n.* 1.
[6] *I.e.* as being still a Deacon.

of his neighbour, doth pass over into the contemplative life through the love of God. The
length of the Stole meaneth perseverance, and
its two ends hanging down are prudence and
temperance ; thus the Apostle saith unto Titus,[1]
LET US LIVE SOBERLY, RIGHTEOUSLY, AND
GODLY, IN THIS PRESENT WORLD. But
according to a decree of the Council of Braga,[2]
the Priest ought with one and the same Stole,
disposing it equally round his neck and both
his shoulders, to trace and make ready[3] on his
breast the sign of the Cross, as one who is
bidden to live between good and evil fortunes,
yet is not dismayed ; that men may ever mark
him surrounded with the adornment of virtue
upon either shoulder. And whoso shall do
otherwise, saith the decree, he shall be duly
liable to excommunication. Unless indeed one
might deem this decree to have been repealed

[1] Tit. ii. 12.

[2] The Fourth Council of Braga, c. 3 (A.D. 675). Grat.
Decr. I. Dist. xxiii. c. 9 ('Ecclesiastica'). This refers to the
Priest who is about to celebrate Mass. The Stole was of
course never crossed in this way until it had become contracted
in size. Bishops and Priests alike formerly wore it pendent on
both sides, as do Bishops now.

[3] Durandus has 'preparare.' In the canon it is 'preparet';
but there is another reading 'praeferat,' 'bear before him the
Sign of the Cross,' which seems much more natural.

by the general custom of the Church to the contrary[1]; for it is not everywhere that the two arms of the Stole are thus disposed upon the breast in the form of a cross. He beareth, then, the Cross on his breast, the while in his heart he taketh pattern by the Passion of Christ, Whose servant he is.

4. The Stole, as I have said, is at once a yoke and a burthen. It is a yoke, that is, unto the Priest, and a burthen unto the Deacon ; and by reason of this the Priest weareth it around his neck, but the Deacon over his left shoulder. For on the neck a yoke is worn, but a burthen is carried upon the shoulder. And if thou read in Leviticus, thou wilt see that the Levites only were appointed unto the bearing of the burthens. Unto the Deacon the Stole signifieth also a yoke, as I have shewn in another Book.[2] And it is placed upon his left

---

[1] From this it appears likely that the present custom, which is in accordance with the Decree, was not very prevalent in Durandus' time. This seems strange, for it has been usual since about the ninth century, as is testified by ancient representations, and discoveries of the Stole in tombs crossed over the breast. However, Durandus says below (§ 5) that ' upon Bishop and Priest it falleth down upon either side evenly.'

[2] 'When he is ordained, the Deacon receiveth the Stole, which signifieth the yoke of Christ, because it will pertain unto him to read the Gospel, wherewith he is encompassed as with a yoke.' (*Rat.* Lib. II. ' De Diacono.')

shoulder, because it is meet that temporal things should be subject unto things spiritual ; or else because it behoveth the right shoulder of the Deacon to be unencumbered, to the end that he may go hither and thither the more freely in the service of the Priest ; whereof also I have already treated, in that place aforesaid.

5. It is girt round at the loins, that the Priest may be strong and active against the onslaughts of lust. But sometimes its forepart is folded over the left arm only ; and this is drawn from the Priests of the Law, who while they sacrificed used to turn back the ends of the girdle over their shoulders.[1] But upon the Bishop or Priest it falleth down before on either side evenly, because Christ, Whose likeness they bear, and Who kept an even mind in weal and woe—which are denoted by right and left—did desire to lead the dwellers of the earth unto heavenly things, and did ever bear this thought before the eyes of His mind.

6. The Stole is also called Orarium, the Praying-Vestment[2] ; because, whereas it is lawful

---

[1] So Josephus, *Ant.* Lib. III. c. 11 : ' When they prepare for the ministry of sacrifice, they carry their girdles on the left shoulder, so as not to be hindered.'

[2] This etymology of the word (*oro*, to pray) is assigned by the Fourth Council of Toledo (c. 28 ; A.D. 633). But it bears

to baptise, to confirm, and to do many other things which stand in prayer, without the other Vestments, yet without the Stole it is lawful to do none of these things, save when driven by urgent need. At the Council of Tribur [1] it was appointed that Priests should not walk, save when vested with the Stole.

It is to be noted, that the Stole was originally a white garment flowing down to the feet, such as the Patriarchs wore before the Law. This was put on by firstborn sons when they received their father's blessing ; on which occasions they offered victims unto God, as though they had been priests. But when the Albe began to be worn, the Stole was altered into the form of a collar. For by the first Stole was understood

the look of being what Bingham calls an 'ecclesiastical deriva-tion,' and is hardly probable. There was a post-classical *orarium*, a handkerchief, which was derived from *os*. 'Oculum ligauit orario ' (S. Aug. *Civ. Dei*, xxii. 8, *no.* 7). This was used for wiping the face (ἐκμαγεῖον τοῦ προσώπου). *Vide* Du Cange, *sub voce*. From a scholar's point of view this etymology is far more satisfactory than either *oro* or *ora*.

[1] A.D. 895. Burchardus, lib.. vi. c. '*Presbyteri.*' The Stole seems to have been the invariable everyday garment of Bishops and Priests until quite a late date. The Council of Mayence (A.D. 813) ordered that priests should wear it 'constantly.' S. Thomas of Canterbury always wore his Stole. Martene quotes these verses of S. Maur, Abbot :

> 'Deponendo Stolam, quam toto tempore caram
> Anni portabat.'

innocence, which was the estate of the first man.
But when he lost his innocence through sin, it
needed that he should recover it as it were
through the Fatted Calf. It remaineth, then,
that we, who fell through disobedience, should
by obedience rise up again ; wherefore we do
rightly bow our necks unto the collar of
obedience, that we may win back the robe of
innocence.[1] For by the Stole which now we
wear, we do accept the obedience of the Gospel
of the Crucified.

7. As touching that which agreeth unto the
Head, even Christ, the Stole, as lying over the
Amice on the Priest's neck, doth signify that
obedience and servitude which the Lord of all
things underwent in order to the salvation of
His own. For He, BEING IN THE FORM OF

[1] The thought is involved. Durandus seems to transfer in
fancy the primal innocence of Adam to the patriarchs, who were
wont, he says, upon receiving their father's blessing, to put on
a large garment called a Stole or robe, and to sacrifice to the
Lord in token that their innocence claimed such blessing as a
right. Whereas for fallen man the birthright can only be
regained through the Sacrifice of Christ, symbolised by the
Fatted Calf, and the Stole with which he is invested is now a
yoke, suggestive of his willingness to submit to that allegiance
which alone shall win him back the garment of righteousness.
Though he does not mention it, Durandus seems to be thinking
of the ' best robe,' which so many Fathers, from Irenaeus downwards, interpret as the robe of righteousness, as put upon the
Prodigal by his Father.

GOD, THOUGHT IT NOT ROBBERY TO BE
EQUAL WITH GOD; BUT MADE HIMSELF OF
NO REPUTATION, AND TOOK UPON HIM THE
FORM OF A SERVANT, AND BECAME OBE-
DIENT UNTO DEATH, EVEN THE DEATH OF
THE CROSS.[1]   Yet did He neither inherit
originally, nor commit actually, aught worthy of
death.

The Stole is also a figure of the band, wherewith Jesus was tied to the column.

8. It hath been appointed[2] in the Canons,
that Subdeacons, Readers, and Singing-Men
may not wear Stoles.

[1] Phil. ii. 6, 7, 8.

[2] In Conc. Laodic. can. 22 and 23 (A.D. 361): οὐ δεῖ
ὑπηρέτην (the Subdeacon) ὠράριον φορεῖν . . . οὐ δεῖ ἀναγνώστας
ἢ ψάλτας ὡρ. φορεῖν.   The Vestment which the Subdeacons
were to wear was the Tunicle; the Stole was the mark of
Bishops and Priests. (Grat. *Decr.* I. Dist. xxiv. c. 'Non
oportet.')   The office of the Readers (lectores) was to take care
of the Sacred Books, and to read the Scriptures in Church; that
of the Psalmist or Cantor, to precent and sing.

CHAPTER VI

OF THE MANIPLE

1. Of the Maniple and its meaning.—2. Why the Maniple is worn upon the left arm.—3. Of the origin thereof.—4, 5. Of the Maniple as touching Christ.—6. Of the Maniple as not worn by the Sacred Ministers, the while they assist the Bishop when he vesteth.

1. FORASMUCH as there is a weariness which often creepeth upon minds well disposed and

---

[1] This Vestment was called indifferently *manipulus*, *mappula*, *sudarium*, and *phanon*; though the two latter were strictly speaking names of quite distinct Vestments, as will be seen in Chs. ix. and xvi. The Maniple was originally merely a napkin for wiping the hands, carried on the arm, especially at Mass. After the sixth century it passed, like many other Vestments, from an utilitarian to a ceremonial purpose. Its ornamental use seems to have been at first confined to the Roman clergy. S. Gregory the Great allowed the chief Deacons of the Church of Ravenna to wear the Maniple while attending on the Bishop at Mass, as a great concession (L. ii. *Ep.* 54 and 55). The Maniple was anciently worn on the hand, rather than on the arm; Archbishop Stigand is so represented in the Bayeux Tapestry. It is now worn by Bishop, Priest, Deacon, and Subdeacon, on the left arm; it varies in colour and texture with the Chasuble, and, like the Chasuble, is discarded for processions.

had in hand for Divine Worship, rendering them
slumbrous with a kind of sluggishness, as saith
the Psalmist,[1] MY SOUL MELTETH AWAY FOR
VERY HEAVINESS ; therefore in the left hand of
the minister who approacheth unto the service
of the Altar is placed a Maniple, which is also
called a Sudarium ; as that he may wipe away
the sweats of his mind and shake off his heart's
heaviness, keeping the watch of good works and
driving weariness and slumber from him.   For
the Maniple is a figure of good works and
watchfulness, whereof the Lord saith, WATCH,
FOR YE KNOW NOT THE HOUR WHEREIN
THE SON OF MAN COMETH[2]; and the Spouse
in the Canticles,[3] I SLEEP, BUT MINE HEART
WAKETH.   As a Sudarium it also denoteth
penitence, wherewith the stain of daily indulgence and the weariness of worldly life are
wiped away ; as it is said, MY SOUL MELTETH
AWAY FOR VERY HEAVINESS[4] ; for the knowledge of sins, and the weakness of the flesh, are
a weariness unto the soul.

The Maniple signifieth also the reward of
future blessings.   Thus in certain places they
wear this Vestment, whose name signifieth also

---

[1] Ps. cxix. 28. [2] S. Matth. xxv. 13.
[3] Cant. v. 2. [4] Ps. cxix. 28.

a sheaf,[1] on Festivals whensoever Albes are used, to show that in that life each one shall receive his due reward ; for THEY SHALL COME AGAIN WITH JOY, BRINGING THEIR SHEAVES WITH THEM.[2]

The Sudarium of the Subdeacon is made greater than that of the Priest, for where there is greater transgression, there is required more fruit of repentance.[3] But of the Sudarium I will speak again.

2. The Ministers wear the Maniple upon the left arm, to show that they must be bound up as touching earthly things, but untrammelled unto heavenly. They of old were not thus bound, for they served God, not only for spiritual, but also for temporal ends. But we in this life, whereof the left hand is a type, do undergo the irksomeness as it were of much sweating, that is, of pleasure, and other excesses of the mind. The Maniple, hanging upon the

---

[1] Lat. *manipulus*, a handful : hence a small bundle of corn, or sheaf; also a 'hand-thing,' in our sense of the Maniple. The word also means a band of soldiers, as we should say a handful of men, or because of the handful of straw on the pole which in primitive times served for a military standard.

[2] Lat. *manipulos*—Ps. cxxvi. 6. A kind of *paronomasia*, or play upon words.

[3] *I.e.* as ideally supposing virtue to increase in the measure of ecclesiastical rank.

E

left arm, denoteth also the faith, which in this life we must have.

3. The use of the Maniple was not taken from Aaron, but from the ancient Fathers of the Church ; as it is written in the Martyrology of Bede, that Arsenius [1] did ever bear a kerchief in his bosom or his hand, to wipe away the abundance of his tears. The holy Fathers also, while they handled the sacred things and celebrated the Sacraments, had little napkins or handkerchiefs on their hands, sometimes to wipe their hands, and sometimes for covering or reverently handling the things of God.

4. As touching that which agreeth unto the Head,[2] even Christ, the wearing of the Maniple on the left hand denoteth this, that Christ won His Prize while in the way ; for, as I have said, the Maniple signifieth a prize, as in that Scripture, THEY SHALL COME AGAIN WITH JOY, BRINGING THEIR SHEAVES WITH THEM ; and the left hand is this present life, as it is written, HIS LEFT HAND IS UNDER MY HEAD, AND

---

[1] Arsenius, called the 'Great,' was one of the most famous of the monks of Egypt. With great asceticism and rigorous sternness of character he combined deep penitence for sin. A mediaeval Collect in commemoration of him speaks of his 'ceaseless floods of tears' (A.D. c. 354–450).

[2] The passage following strikes me as one of singular beauty.

HIS RIGHT HAND DOTH EMBRACE ME.[1] For Christ did enjoy His reward at one and the same time that He was earning it ; He enjoyed it in His own land, and did merit it on His way thither, compassing His prize the while he ran His course, in that He was at once in His native land and on the way to it : as he said, NO MAN HATH ASCENDED UP TO HEAVEN, BUT HE THAT CAME DOWN FROM HEAVEN, EVEN THE SON OF MAN WHICH IS IN HEAVEN.[2]

5. The Maniple is also a figure of the rope with which Jesus was bound, after that He was taken by the Jews, as saith Saint John,[3] THEY TOOK HIM, AND BOUND HIM.

This Vestment is wont to be put upon the Holy Father after the Chasuble,[4] and there be many Bishops beside, who observe this.

---

[1] Cant. ii. 6.   [2] S. John iii. 13.   [3] *Ibid.* xviii. 12.

[4] All Bishops now put on the Maniple after the *Confiteor*, after the Chasuble. Pugin says that formerly the great Chasuble hung down all round the Bishop, and he struck his breast at the ' Meâ Culpâ ' beneath its folds. Then the ministers raised it, folded it back over his arm, and affixed the Maniple. However, Durandus confines this to the Roman Pontiff, and says elsewhere that in his time Bishops put it on *before* the *Confiteor*. These are his words, in effect :—' The Bishop, ere he say *Confiteor*, hath the Maniple put upon him by the Subdeacon, before the Altar. This for three reasons. First, because he must receive and administer temporal goods, not through his own hands, but through the hands of another.

E 2

6. It is to be noted, that the Deacon and Subdeacon, in assisting the Bishop to put on the Sacred Vestments, wear not the Maniple; first, that they may do their parts with the more ease and freedom; and secondly because in the discharge of such a duty they ought not to look for temporal guerdon; which latter is one of the meanings of the Maniple, as I have shown from that of the Psalmist, THEY SHALL COME AGAIN WITH JOY, BRINGING THEIR SHEAVES WITH THEM. And while the Bishop putteth the Vestments on and off, the Deacon

---

Secondly, because confession with the lips sufficeth not, save it be followed by the fruit of good works. Thirdly, that he may be made humble of heart, when he findeth him arrayed with the badge of an inferior ministry. The Bishop, again, putteth on the Maniple after the Chasuble, because Christ, Whose vicegerent he is, did live an heavenly life, or ever He might win to the reward of His labour. But the Priest putteth on the Maniple first, for that he cannot attain unto heavenly conversation, unless he first bear the sheaves of holy works. Wherefore also the Bishop receiveth the Maniple after that he is come to the Altar, in token that we shall then at length receive the reward of our labour, when we are come to the tribunal of the Eternal Judge.' (*Rat.* iv. 7). But the Maniple was *anciently* assumed by Priests as well as Bishops *after* the *Confiteor*. Martene says that in a MS. of the Monastery of S. Denis, written in Charlemagne's time, there occurs after the prayer for putting on the Chasuble, the following prayer for the Maniple :—' Praecinge me, Domine, uirtute, et pone immaculatam uiam meam.'

standeth at his right, and the Subdeacon at his left; for the Deacon, by virtue of his Order, taketh that mightier and higher place than the Subdeacon, which is signified by the right hand.

CHAPTER VII

OF THE CHASUBLE

1. Of the Chasuble : its name and meaning.—2. Of Charity, as set forth in the Chasuble.—3. Of the folds of the Chasuble, and what they signify.—4. Of the same ; and of the Chasuble as touching Christ.—5. Of the Chasuble as whole and enclosed, and what it signifieth.

1. LASTLY, over all the Vestments the Priest putteth on the Chasuble,[1] which is being interpreted a 'little cottage.' It is called by the Greeks the Planet, from *Plane*, a wandering, for that its border wandereth [2] wide as it is raised

---

[1] The word is derived from *casula*, a little house. So S. Isidore (*c.* A.D. 600), who explains that 'like a hut, it covers the entire person' (*De Origin.* xix. cap. 21). It is called also *amphibalum*, *planeta*, and *paenula*. It seems to have been a somewhat humble garment at first, being confined to peasants and artisans ; and it had a hood, as a protection against the weather. It was long the ordinary outdoor dress of the clergy and monks, before it passed into the present ecclesiastical Vestment, so indispensable to, and characteristic of, the Holy Sacrifice of the Altar. The Council of Ratisbon (A.D. 742) directs that Priests and Deacons shall wear the 'Casula' out of doors.

[2] So Isidore, *De Etymol.* xix. 24. But some ascribe this

over the arms, signifying Charity, without which
the Priest is as a SOUNDING BRASS, OR AS A
TINKLING CYMBAL.[1] For as Charity covereth
THE MULTITUDE OF SINS,[2] and containeth all
the commandments of the Law and the Prophets,
and is called by the Apostle,[3] THE FULFILLING
OF THE LAW ; so also this Vestment wandereth
over all, and doth enclose and contain all other
Vestments within itself.[4]

name to its starlike appearance when folded back. The name
is used more strictly of the *folded*-chasuble. (Dr. Littledale
thought that the Planeta is represented now by the Chasuble,
and the Casula or Casacula by the Cassock.)

[1] 1 Cor. xiii. 1.   [2] 1 S. Pet. iv. 8.

[3] Rom. xiii. 10.

[4] The primitive Chasuble, being quite round, enveloped the
whole body. Certain schools sigh for this 'ancient perfection'
of the Chasuble, with its 'graceful folds.' How it can be
possible to desire the renewal of so cumbersome a garment,
with its sides continually slipping over the hands, to the
great peril of the Holy Sacrifice in both paten and chalice ;
or what especial dignity or beauty can reside in a mere circle
of cloth with a hole in the middle for the head, it is hard to
conceive. Were the human figure spherical, it would be all
that could be desired. It was appropriate in its own time and
place. But there is such a thing as 'old-fashion' in the Church
as in the world. We do not revive ordinary garments after
they have become unsuitable ; and there are few sights so
ludicrous or so unbecoming the dignity of Divine worship as
that of a short Priest in an enormous Chasuble. It is not well
that their prevailing horror of 'modern Romanism' should
drive Englishmen to absurdities. Moreover, antiquarian punc-
tilio is apt to forget that external matters, in the Church, are
subject to development. Surely the almost universal adoption

2. Of charity also the Apostle saith,[1] YET SHOW I UNTO YOU A MORE EXCELLENT WAY. THOUGH I SPEAK WITH THE TONGUES OF MEN AND OF ANGELS, AND HAVE NOT CHARITY, I AM NOTHING. And again, THOUGH I HAVE ALL FAITH, SO THAT I COULD REMOVE MOUNTAINS, AND HAVE NOT CHARITY, I AM NOTHING.[1] The Chasuble, moreover, is the Wedding-Garment spoken of by the Lord in the Gospel,[2] FRIEND, HOW CAMEST THOU IN HITHER, NOT HAVING ON A WEDDING-GAR-MENT? Without this, the Priest may never discharge his office, for it beseemeth him ever to abide in the bond of charity.

The Amice goeth round the mouth of the Chasuble, which meaneth that good works ought

of a smaller form of this and of other Vestments by the great Latin Church is more authoritative and more convincing than the private 'fads' of scholars, who forget that logical consistence demands of them the rejection of the whole principle of ritual evolution, and a return, along the entire range of worship, to the models of whatever century they happen to have honoured with their preference. Surely in these, as in greater matters, the Holy Spirit was to 'guide into all truth'; and to appeal from the Holy Ghost in the nineteenth century to the Holy Ghost in the first, or second, or thirteenth, whether in things great or small, is dangerously near to stultifying that promise of perpetual guidance. Antiquarianism is a good thing. But Antiquarianism in conflict with Catholicism helped to produce the Anabaptist heresy.

[1] 1 Cor. xiii. 1 and 2.   [2] S. Matth. xxii. 12.

always to have charity for their source and end.[1]
For THE END OF THE COMMANDMENT IS
CHARITY OUT OF A PURE HEART, AND OF
A GOOD CONSCIENCE, AND OF FAITH UN-
FEIGNED.[2] And the dividing of the Chasuble
√ into two parts, back and fore, when the Priest
extendeth his hands, signifieth the two arms of
charity, wherewith it reacheth unto God, and to
his neighbour, as in that Scripture,[3] THOU
SHALT LOVE THE LORD THY GOD, AND THY
NEIGHBOUR AS THYSELF; ON THESE TWO
COMMANDMENTS HANG ALL THE LAW AND
THE PROPHETS.   Again, the wideness of the
Chasuble is a figure of the breadth of Charity,
which reacheth even as far as our enemies;
whence it is written, THY COMMANDMENT IS
EXCEEDING BROAD.[4]

   3. The Chasuble hath two folds, right and
left[5]; these be the two precepts of charity, the

[1] 'Bonum opus debet ad charitatem referri.'
[2] 1 Tim. i. 5.
[3] S. Matth. xxii. 37-40.   [4] Ps. cix. 96.
[5] Durandus doubtless means the natural gathering of the
Vestment over the arms on each side, to leave the hands free.
This, of course, necessitated a limp material, for it would have
been impossible with our thickly-embroidered Vestments. The
raising of the Chasuble on either side by the Ministers, which
was then necessary to free the Priest's hands for censing, etc.,
survives now only ceremonially.   In Durandus' time it had
developed from its primitive circular shape into that of a vesica,

love of God, and the love of his neighbour. Also it is folded double across the breast,[1] which meaneth the heart, and between the shoulders, which are good works ; in these parts, I say, the Chasuble is made to double upon itself, for we ought so to show good deeds unto our neighbour outwardly, that we may keep the same within, whole in the heart before God. For we need to have charity in our heart, and in our work ; both within and without. It is doubled before the breast, again, because by charity are gotten goodwill and holy thought ; and between the shoulders, because by charity are borne untoward dealings of neighbours and adversaries. And it is lifted up at the arms, as when we work the good works of love : at the right arm, as when we DO GOOD UNTO THEM WHO ARE OF THE HOUSEHOLD OF FAITH[2];

which hung down in long points when the arms were raised, behind and before. The effect of this must have been very graceful.

[1] So also Honorius, Bishop of Autun. It is not obvious what kind of ' doubling ' is referred to. Durandus may (i.) be referring to the folded-chasuble, or to the ancient practice of throwing back the borders of the Planeta for convenience before celebrating ; or (ii.) perhaps the Chasuble was made of a double thickness in the regions named (though he says below that it was ' of one piece ') ; but more probably (iii.) the natural folds of the Vestment are meant, which would be caused by the raising of the arms.

[2] Gal. vi. 10.

and at the left, as when our righteous dealings reach even unto our enemies.

4. Furthermore, over the arms it maketh √three folds[1]; on the right arm, as when we succour the faithful, monks, clergy, and laity; and on the left, as when we minister to the needs of unbelievers, that is, bad Christians, Jews, and paynim. For well are works of righteousness symbolised by the Chasuble, according unto this Scripture,[2] LET THY PRIESTS BE CLOTHED WITH RIGHTEOUSNESS. The Priest may not put off his Chasuble while he performeth his office; for the Lord commandeth in the twenty-first chapter of Leviticus,[3] that HE SHALL NOT GO OUT OF THE SANCTUARY, that is, out of holy things or commandments.

Further, as touching that which agreeth unto the Head, even Christ, the Chasuble of the Great Priest is the Catholic Church, concerning which the Apostle[4] saith, AS MANY OF YOU AS

---

[1] Doubtless this refers to the natural folds upon the raised arms.

[2] Ps. cxxxii. 9.   [3] Lev. xxi. 12.

[4] Gal. iii. 27. So Rupert, Bishop of Tuy, in his comments *De Divinis Officiis*. It will be observed that Durandus says nothing about the orfreys or ornamentation of the Chasuble, and does not allude to the Y cross upon it. Yet this undoubtedly existed in his time. Agnellus, in his Life of S. Maximian, who was Bishop of Ravenna in the sixth century,

HAVE BEEN BAPTISED INTO CHRIST HAVE PUT ON CHRIST. This is that Vestment of Aaron, unto whose skirt the ointment ran down: IT RAN DOWN FROM HIS HEAD UNTO HIS BEARD, AND FROM HIS BEARD UNTO THE SKIRTS OF HIS CLOTHING IT RAN DOWN.[1] For OF THE FULNESS OF HIS SPIRIT HAVE WE ALL RECEIVED,[2] first the Apostles, then they that are come after them.

5. The Chasuble is of one piece, and whole, and is hemmed on every side, which signifieth the unity and wholeness of the Faith. Yet when the Priest spreadeth out his hands, it is in a manner divided in two parts, back and fore; and this denoteth the ancient Church, which went before the Passion of Christ, and the new, which followeth it; for THE MULTITUDES THAT WENT BEFORE, AND THAT FOLLOWED, CRIED, SAYING, HOSANNA TO THE SON OF

says that Maximian had an altar-cloth embroidered with pictures of his predecessors, and that these Bishops were depicted as wearing Chasubles with the 'auriclave' in front, in shape like the Pallium, which is thus (Y). It is well known that this cross represents the raising of Our Blessed Lord's arms in the Crucifixion, and that the straight orfrey often found on the front of the Chasuble is symbolical of the stake to which He was bound when scourged. These significations are of course instances of the evolution of symbolism from utility.

[1] Ps. cxxxiii. 2.   S. John i. 16.

DAVID : BLESSED IS HE THAT COMETH IN THE NAME OF THE LORD.[1]

This Vestment representeth also the purple robe with which the soldiers encompassed Christ, as saith John in the nineteenth chapter.[2]

[1] S. Matth. xxi. 9.   [2] S. John xix. 2.

CHAPTER VIII

OF THE BUSKINS AND SANDALS

1. Why the feet be clad in Vestments.—2. When and why the Bishop putteth on the Buskins and Sandals.—3, 4. Of the Buskins and Sandals, their counsel and warning.—5. Of the Sandals : why they be so called, and the meaning thereof. 6. Why they be open in some parts, and closed in others. 7. Of the matter and colour thereof.—8, 9. Of the latchet and strings of the Sandals.—10. Of the Sandals as touching Christ.—11. Concerning those who may, and those who may not, wear the Sandals.

1. In the foregoing we have spoken of the six Vestments common to both Bishops and Priests. It now remaineth to treat of the nine that are peculiar to the Bishop. And first let us consider the Buskins and Sandals.

The vesting of the feet taketh not its beginning from Aaron's line of Priests, for they lived in Jewry, and therefore had no need thereof; but from the Apostles, unto whom it was said, GO YE AND TEACH ALL NATIONS.[1] Unless indeed one might say that the Buskins

---

[1] S. Matth. xxviii. 19.

and Sandals take the place of the breeches of the ancient Priest.

2. The Bishop, then, being about to cele-brate, while the five appointed Psalms [1] are said, putteth on the Buskins and Sandals, the PREPARATION OF THE GOSPEL OF PEACE.[2] These are they which for beauty the Prophet did laud, saying, HOW BEAUTIFUL ARE THE FEET OF THEM THAT BRING GOOD TIDINGS OF PEACE, THAT PUBLISH GOOD TIDINGS OF GOOD![3] and the Apostle, saying unto the Ephesians, HAVING YOUR FEET SHOD WITH THE PREPARATION OF THE GOSPEL OF PEACE.[4] And in the Gospel we read that the Lord sent His disciples forth shod with sandals[5]—shod indeed, that is, with the PREPARATION OF THE GOSPEL OF PEACE ; for if they had not been thus shod, how could they have trodden upon serpents and scorpions ?[6]

3. Let Bishops take thought, therefore, why they are thus shod, and let them copy the example of those, whose sandals they copy. For the feet are a fit type of the affections;

---

[1] As ordered in the Roman Missal. According to the Prayer Book computation, they are Pss. lxxxiv., lxxxv., lxxxvi., cxvi. (or [?] to end) and cxxv.

[2] Eph. vi. 15.   [3] Is. lii. 7.   [4] Eph. vi. 15.
[5] S. Mark vi. 9.   [6] S. Luke x. 19.

wherefore they ought to have sandals, so to speak, upon their affections and desires, that they be not stained with the dust of things earthly or temporal.

4. By these Sandals we do also meetly understand a check, put upon the feet, lest they hasten unto forbidden things. And whereas a man's affections become more readily tainted and marred in time of prosperity, which is signified by the right hand, than in time of adversity, which is exprest by the left, the Bishop doth put the sandal on his right foot first, to show that one ought to run the quicker, to meet the greater danger.

But before the Sandals are put on the feet, they are clad in Buskins, [1] reaching so far as the knee and there girt round, for that the preacher ought to MAKE STRAIGHT PATHS FOR HIS FEET, AND CONFIRM THE FEEBLE KNEES [2];

[1] *Caligae*, called also *Compagi*. These are a kind of stocking of some precious material, quite distinct from the Sandals, and reaching to the knee, where they are fastened. Sicardus of Cremona (twelfth century) says that they were of silk. They were originally peculiar to the Pope, but towards the ninth century seem to have become an universal Episcopal Vestment. The earliest writer who mentions 'caligae' as regularly included in the Sacred Vestments to be worn by Bishops and Cardinals is Ivo Carnotensis (c. A.D. 1115).

[2] Heb. xii. 12, 13.

for HE THAT SHALL DO AND TEACH THESE
COMMANDMENTS, THE SAME SHALL BE
CALLED THE GREATEST IN THE KINGDOM OF
HEAVEN.[1] And the Buskins, being of blue,[2]
the colour of the firmament, denote that his
feet—that is, his affections—must be heavenly,
and strong, that he halt not ; but that he may
SAY TO THEM THAT ARE OF A FEARFUL
HEART, BE STRONG.[3]

5. After these, his feet are vested in the
Sandals,[4] which are so called from the plant of
that name, or from sandarach,[5] wherewith they

[1] S. Matth. v. 19.

[2] Sometimes crimson, sometimes cloth of gold. The
Buskins found in the tomb of Boniface VIII. were of black silk.

[3] Is. xxxv. 4.

[4] It appears that no mention of the Sandals as a distinctively
Episcopal Vestment occurs before the ninth century, unless
S. Gregory, in forbidding Deacons to wear 'sandalia' (L. vii.
Ep. 28), be speaking of them. They were originally worn by
all Holy Orders, as might be expected from their purely secular
origin. Amalarius says they were worn by Priests as late as
the ninth century (*De Eccles. Offic.* L. li. c. 25). They
were often embroidered in the most costly manner. In old
representations they are generally red, but sometimes purple,
or white.

[5] *Sandaraca,* σανδαράκη, a red mineral colouring matter ;
(Vitr. vii. 12, 2 ; Du Cange, *sub voce*). But the derivation is
improbable, as there is also a Persian word *sandal.* The
Greek word σάνδαλον is more probably connected with σανίς,
a wooden board, as being a sole of wood for the foot.
Durandus' alternative derivation, 'the plant of that name,' is

F

are coloured. Now these have an entire sole underneath, but on the top there is latticed hide ; because the steps of the Preacher ought to be guarded from beneath, lest they be defiled with earthly things, as saith the Lord, SHAKE OFF THE DUST OF YOUR FEET ;[1] but they must be open above, that they may be unveiled unto the knowledge of heavenly mysteries, according unto that of the Psalmist,[2] OPEN THOU MINE EYES, THAT I MAY SEE THE WONDROUS THINGS OF THY LAW. They are open on the top, again, because we ought to have hearts ever uplifted unto God, and our minds' eyes open unto those things which be above : and solid beneath, because we must keep a mind impervious amid earthly things, and seek the blessing, not of Esau, which is earthly, but of Jacob, which is in the heavens.

6. The Sandals again, being open in certain places and closed in others, signify that the preaching of the Gospel ought neither to be revealed unto all, nor hid from all, as it is written, UNTO YOU IT IS GIVEN TO KNOW THE

not obvious. There was a *white* kind of corn mentioned by Pliny, called *sandala*, and a kind of palm called *sandalis* ; but it is difficult to connect either with the sandal.

[1] S. Matth. x. 14.   [2] Ps. cxix. 18.

MYSTERIES OF THE KINGDOM OF GOD, BUT
UNTO OTHERS IN PARABLES.[1] And GIVE NOT
THAT WHICH IS HOLY UNTO THE DOGS,
NEITHER CAST YE YOUR PEARLS BEFORE
SWINE.[2]

7. The inner part of the Sandals is sometimes made of white leather, for it needeth to
have a clean intention, and a conscience pure
before God; and without there is a dark
appearance, because the life of the preacher
seemeth dark and mean in worldly eyes, by
reason of the trials of this world. Sometimes
too they are red, to signify the spirit of martyrdom; and at other times they are variegated
with divers colours, the manifold virtues wherewith we need to be adorned.

8. A latchet, which is separate from the
leather, goeth up over the foot, and figureth the
tongues of those who bear good testimony unto
the preacher, but who are nevertheless separate
in a manner from the conversation of spiritual
men. In the second place, this latchet is itself
the tongue of the spiritual, which did induct the
preacher into the office of preaching. Thirdly,
it denoteth also the tongue of the preacher
himself. The line which runneth from this

[1] S. Luke viii. 10.   [2] S. Matth. vii. 6.

F 2

latchet through the midst of the Sandal unto
the end thereof, is Evangelical Perfection ; and
the lines which come forth from either side,
and which at the end of the Sandal run into
that middle line and there have an end, are a
figure of the Law and the Prophets, which be
ratified in the Gospel, and there find the end of
their being. The upper part of the Sandal,
into which the foot is placed, is joined together
with divers strings, that its two sides slip not
away nor be parted, coming unfastened the one
from the other ; and this is to show that the
Preacher ought to bind himself with divers
virtues, or truths of Scripture, that his inner
part may not be disjoined from that which
shineth without, in the sight of the Most High.
Also the very fastening of the Sandals signifieth that the prelate, who hath to go hither
and thither, ought to make sure his mind's
steps, the while he goeth to and fro amid the
throng.

9. The drawing of the thongs this way and
that with the hands, in binding and making
fast the Sandals, signifieth that the Priest ought
to walk with so firm a step, that he may be a
burthen unto none nor faint in the way of his
ministry. For it is in vain if he run fast who

fainteth or ever he reacheth the goal ; inasmuch
as the Sandals do mystically represent the race
of the Preacher. But sometimes they are not
fastened, for that Christ's Incarnation is in
some measure open unto human understanding,
as we may understand the being wrapt in
garments, or placed in an enclosure. Sometimes, again, the cost of the thongs is over and
above that of the Sandals, as it is written,
WHATSOEVER THOU SPENDEST MORE, WHEN
I COME AGAIN I WILL REPAY THEE.[1]

It may also be said that the Buskins are a
type of that washing, of which the Lord said,
HE THAT IS BATHED NEEDETH NOT SAVE
TO WASH HIS FEET.[2] But, for that cleanness
of heart sufficeth not without patience in
persecution, they have also stripes of red,[3]
which are a type of martyrdom. Thus he that
hath cleanness in his heart, and patience, an it
so needeth, in his will, shall come secure unto
the office of preaching, which the apostolic
Sandals signify.

10. Further, as touching that which agreeth

---

[1] S. Luke x. 35.
[2] S. John xiii. 10.   See Chap. xix. of this work, p. 165, *n.* 2.
[3] *Centones rubei.* 'Cento' usually means patchwork. It
probably refers here to the red cross sometimes found on a
white sandal.

unto the Head, even Christ, the Sandals have
another meaning.   The Bishop, who in the
service of the Altar representeth the Person of
Christ his Head, Whose member he is; the
while he putteth the Sandals on his feet, doth
suggest the Lord putting on those Sandals of
the Incarnation, whereof He saith in the Psalms,[1]
OVER EDOM WILL I CAST OUT MY SHOE, that
is, 'among the nations will I make known my
Incarnation.' For the Godhead came unto us
as it were sandalled, that for us the Son of God
might discharge the Priestly office.   And by
the latchets wherewith the Sandals are fastened
upon the feet, we do understand that same
mystery which John the Baptist saw in the
sandal-strings, when he said, WHOSE SHOE'S
LATCHET I AM NOT WORTHY TO UNLOOSE:[2]
that is, the unspeakable union and indissoluble
bond of flesh whereby the Godhead of the Word
did join itself with humanity of ours.   Moreover,
the feet are united with the Sandals by the
mediation of the Buskins, which are worn
between; and this pictureth the union of the
Human Soul with the Godhead, through the
mean of Flesh.   For as the foot beareth up the

---

[1] Ps. lx. 8.   [2] S. John i. 27.

body, even so the Godhead governeth the world.[1]
Thus the Psalmist[2] saith, FALL DOWN BEFORE
HIS FOOTSTOOL, FOR HE IS HOLY.

11. According to a decree of Gregory,[3]
Deacons may not wear 'compagi,' that is,
Sandals, nor 'maniples,' that is, episcopal shoes,
without special licence of the Apostolic See.
Formerly they did wear these, because it was
their duty to go hither and thither in attendance.
But nowadays neither Deacons nor Priests wear
these Vestments, but Bishops only, that by this
diversity of their Sandals the distinction of their
office may be marked ; and beside, they have to
go abroad amongst the people, whereas it is the
duty of the Priest to offer the sacrifices of the

---

[1] The sequence of thought is obscure. Durandus seems to
mean one of two things : (i.) that the feet are a type of the
Godhead, and the Sandals of Our Lord's Human Soul. But
the thought of Our Lord's Godhead being united with His
Human Soul through the medium of His Flesh seems strange.
One might have thought rather that His Godhead was united
with His Flesh through the medium of His Soul ; but this, too, is
strained. But the passage more probably means (ii.) that the
feet are the Godhead, and the Sandals man's soul, which is
brought to God by the medium of the Incarnation, typified by
the Buskins.

[2] Ps. xcix. 5.

[3] Grat. *Decret.* I. Dist. xciii. c. 20 (' compagis uero calciari
absque apostolica licentia diaconibus non permittitur, sicut nec
mappulis '). And Greg. ' Ioanni Episcopo Siracusano,' L. vii.
Epist. 28, Indict. I.

Lord. Yet the clerics of the Roman Church, by the indulgence of Constantine, Emperor, might wear shoes with socks [1] of white linen.

[1] ' Et sicut noster senatus calceamentis utitur cum udonibus, idest candido linteamine illustratis, sic utantur et clerici, ut sicut coelestia, ita et terrena ad laudem Dei decorentur.' (' And whereas our senate wear sandals enriched with socks of white linen, let the clergy wear the same, that both heavenly and earthly things may be adorned to the praise of God.') ' Donation of Constantine,' Grat. *Decr.* I. Dist. xcvi. c. 14.

CHAPTER IX

OF THE UNDERGIRDLE AND VEIL

1. Of the Undergirdle; and of the Pope's Orale.—2. Of the Pectoral Cross.

1. As touching the Undergirdle, I will add nought further to such as I have already said in the treating of the Zone or Girdle, in the Proeme[1] of this Book.

The Bishop of Rome after the Albe and Girdle putteth on the Orale,[2] a Vestment of fine stuff, which after the manner of a veil he placeth upon his head, and foldeth it over his shoulders and before his breast; following the

---

[1] See Proeme, § 4, and Chap. iv. throughout, with Notes. In Durandus' time the Undergirdle was the common property of all Bishops, but it is now a Papal Vestment. This chapter is borrowed almost bodily from Innocent III. *De Myst. Miss.* Lib. I. c. 53.

[2] A striped veil like a coloured amice, which the Pope puts on after the Girdle, turned back over the head, until the Chasuble is put on, when it is brought down over the shoulders and breast.

use of the Priest of the Law, who after the broidered coat and girdle did put on the ephod or superhumeral, whose place the Amice doth now take.

The aforesaid Bishop putteth on also a certain Cross,[1] fastened to a fine chain, which he hangeth around his neck, disposing the Cross before his breast. For the High Priest of the Law did wear a golden plate upon his forehead,[2] in the stead of which this High Priest, the Bishop, doth wear the Cross upon his breast ; and so the golden plate yieldeth place unto the Sign of the Cross. For the mystery[3] which the golden plate enshrined in its Four Letters, hath been set forth in four arms by the Sign of the

---

[1] Durandus, with Innocent III. and also S. Thomas, seems to confine the Pectoral Cross to the Pope. It is of course now the common property of all Bishops. Yet in Durandus' time, though not a part of the exclusively Episcopal dress, it was worn by Bishops. Georgius says that Pectoral Crosses were called ἐγκόλπια by the Greeks ; for the practice of wearing a Cross seems to have come from the East, where all the faithful, but especially the Bishops, wore them. The use probably originated in the wearing of a reliquary, containing the wood of the Holy Cross, in the bosom, the reliquary itself becoming cruciform in shape. Nicephorus the Emperor (A.D. 811) sent Pope Leo III. a golden Pectoral Cross, containing relics of the true Cross.

[2] Ex. xxviii. 38.

[3] For this mystery, see Chap. xix., § 16.

Cross; as saith the Apostle,[1] THAT YE MAY BE
ABLE TO COMPREHEND WITH ALL SAINTS
WHAT IS THE BREADTH, AND LENGTH, AND
DEPTH, AND HEIGHT. Wherefore that holy
thing which he then did bear in the plate upon
his brow, his successor doth now hide within
his heart; for WITH THE HEART MAN BE-
LIEVETH UNTO RIGHTEOUSNESS, AND WITH
THE MOUTH CONFESSION IS MADE UNTO
SALVATION.[2] And according to Hierome, 'the
Blood of the Gospel is more precious than the
gold of the Law.' He placeth the Cross before
his breast, again, for the shewing forth of that
which the Apostle saith, GLORIFY GOD AND
BEAR HIM IN YOUR BODY.[3] And when he putteth
the Cross on himself, and when he taketh it off,
he kisseth it, for that he doth believe and
confess Christ's Passion, whereof it is the sign,
and unto whose representation in the Office of
the Mass he maketh him ready.

[1] Eph. iii. 18.　　　　　[2] Rom. x. 10.
[3] 1 Cor. vi. 2, adapted, with a reminiscence of Gal. vi. 17.

CHAPTER X

OF THE TUNIC

1. Of the Tunic and its meaning.—2. Of the two Tunics of the Old Testament, and what they signified ; also of the two Tunics of the Bishop.—3. Of the hue of the Tunic ; and of the Jacinth.—4. Again of the two Tunics of the Bishop. 5. Of the Tunic as touching Christ.

1. AFTER the Stole put on, the Bishop is arrayed in the Tunic, which is otherwise called Subtile,[1] and in the Law, Poderes, that is, the garment which reacheth unto the feet. And this signifieth Perseverance. Thus Joseph is described as having worn such a garment amongst his brethren.[2] For when the other virtues run in the race, Perseverance only receiveth the prize, as it is written, HE THAT PERSEVERETH UNTO THE END, THE SAME

---

[1] The word occurs in Is. xix. 9, Vulg. ('confundentur texentes subtilia ') and Ezek. xvi. 10 ('indui te subtilibus,' LXX τὴν βύσσον).

[2] Gen. xxxvii. 3 (' fecitque ei tunicam polymitam ').

SHALL BE SAVED [1] ; and One teacheth, BE THOU
FAITHFUL UNTO DEATH, AND I WILL GIVE
THEE A CROWN OF LIFE.[2] Again, he putteth
on the Tunic after the Albe, because by the
Albe is figured the chastening of the flesh,
while the Tunic is the symbol of those inner
virtues, which the perfect need alway to have.
The Tunic is not girded, because by reason of
its shape it hindereth not the steps : so also the
virtues that are set forth by it afford a free
walk in the contemplation of God. Yet is the
Albe girded, as I have said in the chapter
which treateth of the Girdle.

2. In the Old Testament there were two
tunics, the tunic of fine linen, and the blue
tunic.[3] And at this day also certain Bishops
use two Tunics,[4] to show that it beseemeth
them to have knowledge of both Testaments,

[1] S. Matth. x. 22.   [2] Rev. ii. 10.

[3] Ex. xxxix. 22 and 27 ; or xxviii. 31 ('tunica superhumeralis,' the Robe of the Ephod) and 39 ('tunica byssina,'
the coat of fine linen).

[4] *I.e.* Dalmatic and Tunicle. The words were almost interchangeable in Durandus' time. In the *Pontificale Ecclesiae
Cameracensis* occurs this prayer, to be said in putting on the
Dalmatic : 'Indue me, Domine, vestimento salutis, *et Tunica
iustitiae.*' And in most old English inventories the two Vestments are called indifferently 'Tunacles.' The early Dalmatic
was a little larger than the Tunicle, and had ampler sleeves.
See following chapter, § 3.

that they may know how to bring out of the
Lord's treasure things new and old [1] ; or that
they may shew themselves that they are both
Deacons and Priests. Besides, each of the
Tunics doth bear his own proper signification.
The white Tunic,[2] which is of fine linen, signi-
fieth Chastity, as may be gathered from what
hath been said in the chapter of the Albe.[3]
This former Tunic, too, if it be of silk, denoteth
Chastity and Humility ; for silk taketh its
beginning from worms, which are created with-
out intercourse.

3. The second Tunic ought to be blue, as in
olden days it was of the colour of the jacinth,
which followeth in its hue the sereneness of the
sky ; wherefore it is a figure of the Saints with
their heavenly thoughts and lives, and of
celestial thought and conversation. For as that
precious stone, the jacinth, doth change his
colour with the changes of the sky, being bright
when the firmament is bright, and pale beneath
a darkling heaven ; even so in spiritual figure
ought the Bishop to REJOICE WITH THEM THAT

---

[1] S. Matth. xiii. 52.
[2] Evidently the Dalmatic, which Pope Silvester ordered to
be of white.
[3] § 1.

DO REJOICE, AND WEEP WITH THEM THAT
WEEP.[1] Yet if the Tunic be of any other colour,
it beareth accordingly some other meaning.

4. And the Bishop weareth the one Tunic
beneath the other, to shew that as that which· is
hid may not be seen of the people, but is known
to the clergy alone, so also that measure of lofty
virtues pictured by it, which the perfect man
ought ever to possess, may not be open to the
eyes of all, but only unto the higher orders, and
unto them that are perfect.

5. Furthermore, as touching that which agreeth
unto the Head, even Christ, this Vestment in
the ancient Priesthood was of blue, and had for
its fringe pomegranates and golden bells hanging from its lower hem, that the High Priest
might walk all in music[2]; as shall be said in
the chapter of the Vestments of the Law.[3] And
this giveth an hint of the heavenly doctrine of
the Christ, Whereof all have taken knowledge;
unto Whom it was said by the Prophet,[4] O
THOU WHO TELLEST GOOD TIDINGS TO SION,
GET THEE UP INTO THE HIGH MOUNTAIN.

---

[1] Rom. xii. 15.

[2] Ex. xxviii. 33-35.   [3] § 10.

[4] Is. xl. 9 (Vulg. 'super montem excelsum ascende, tu qui
euangelizas Sion'—where 'Sion' may be either vocative or
accusative).

More than all, however, had the Weaver of the doctrine of the Gospel this Tunic, the Wisdom of God, Jesus Christ, and gave it unto His Apostles; for ALL THINGS, said He, WHICH I HAVE HEARD OF MY FATHER, I HAVE MADE KNOWN UNTO YOU.[1]   This also was the signification of that Tunic of the Lord, which the soldiers would not rend, for that it was WITH- OUT SEAM, WOVEN FROM THE TOP THROUGH- OUT [2]—as though they thought the Lord's loss would be great; the which sheweth how great a loss they cause who strive to rend with their heresies the doctrines of the Gospel.

The Subdeacon, also, weareth the Tunic, as shall be shewn in the following chapter.

[1] S. John xv. 15.   [2] *Ibid.* xix. 23.

CHAPTER XI

OF THE DALMATIC

1. THE Bishop, immediately after the Tunic, vesteth him in the Dalmatic, according to the institution of Silvester, Pope.[1] This is believed to have been borrowed from the Lord's seamless coat, and from the Colobium of the Apostles.

---

[1] But in the account of the martyrdom of S. Cyprian, long before Pope Silvester's time (which was 315-325 A.D.), we read that S. Cyprian, being led to martyrdom, 'cum se Dalmatica exspoliasset et diaconibus tradidisset, in linea stetit' ('Ex Passione S. Cypr. Pontii Diacon.' in *Act. Mart. sincer.* p. 205, *in fine*). Pope Silvester probably made the Episcopal use of this Vestment general. Walafrid Strabo says that before that Pope's time Bishops and Priests both wore Dalmatics, but that when they began to use Chasubles they allowed Deacons to wear Dalmatics (*De Reb. Eccl.* c. 24). And S. Isidore calls the Dalmatic 'a sacerdotal Vestment.'

G

Now the Colobium [1] is a dress without sleeves,
such as is now seen in the cowl [2] of a monk.
But Pope Silvester changed it into the Dalmatic,
by adding broad sleeves, and ordered it to be
worn at the Sacrifice of the Altar. [3]

2. Now the Dalmatic is so called, because
it was devised [4] in Dalmatia, after all other
priestly Vestments. By its shape it signifieth
liberality, for it hath large sleeves and long.
For according to the Apostle [5] it beseemeth
that a Bishop should be NOT GREEDY OF
FILTHY LUCRE, BUT GIVEN TO HOSPITALITY;

[1] This was a short under-tunic, anciently an under-garment
of the Romans, and worn originally by all freemen, and latterly
by senators. It appears to have been the Vestment of a Deacon
at the time when the Dalmatic distinguished Bishops and
Priests. It is derived from κολοβός, short, or stunted.

[2] The monastic 'cowls' known to Durandus probably
reached to the feet. 'Cuculla quae nostro singulariter con-
venit ordini, quod uestimentum antiquitus uocabatur Colobium,
idest tunica sine manicis, tantum debet habere longitudinis
antea, quod ad callum pedis usque pertingat.' ['The Cowl of
our Order, formerly called Colobium, a tunic without sleeves,
ought to be long enough in front to reach the sole of the foot.']
Guidonis Disciplina Farfensis, cap. 4, 'De uestimentorum
mensura.'

[3] Bingham (*Orig. Eccles.* vol. I. Bk. vi. ch. 4, § 20) says
the Dalmatic was otherwise called χειρόδοτος, or *Tunica
manicata*, because it had these sleeves down to the hands.

[4] *Reperta.* 'Dalmaticas testatur Isidorus Episcopus in
Dalmatia primum contextas' (Onuphrius Panvinus, *Interpr.
Voc. Eccles.*, sub 'Dalm. ; S. Isidore, *Etym.* xix. 22).

[5] Tit. i. 7 and 8.

wherefore he must not have a hand closed from giving and strecht out to receive ; but must do that which the Prophet doth advise, BREAK THY BREAD UNTO THE HUNGRY, AND BRING THE POOR THAT ARE CAST OUT TO THINE HOUSE.[1] And it is on this account, doubtless, that Deacons in especial do wear Dalmatics, for that they chiefly were appointed by the Apostles unto the office of serving tables.

3. Further, the Deacon's Dalmatic hath fuller sleeves than the Tunicle of the Subdeacon, because he himself ought to have a charity ampler than the other, by reason of his greater gift. But the Dalmatic of the Bishop hath wider sleeves than that of the Deacon, to shew that the former is more unhindered, and hath nought that may hold back his hand ; for upon heavenly things he must lavish all, and his charity must reach even unto his adversaries. But the Tunicle of the Subdeacon, the Dalmatic of the Deacon, and the Chasuble of the Priest, do all follow in the stead of the blue Tunic, which was of the colour of the heaven ; in token that all the ministers of the Altar ought to live an heavenly life, according unto higher or lower rank, which are marked by the breadth

[1] Is. lviii. 7.

or straitness of the sleeves of the Dalmatic
and Tunicle respectively, as hath been said
before.

4. The Priest, because he ought to be the
least hindered as touching heavenly things,
weareth not these Vestments, nor indeed aught
else whereby the arms may be straitened.
But the Bishop weareth at once the Dalmatic,
and the Tunic, and the Vestments of all Orders,
to shew that he containeth all Orders in himself
perfectly, as who bestoweth them all upon
other. These the lesser ministers bestow not,
and therefore wear not the Vestments that
figure them, but for them one sufficeth, to sig
nify the heavenly life. Beside, the Bishop,
both in his ornaments and in his Office, beareth
in more special wise the likeness of the Saviour
than doth the simple Priest, and the significations of the Vestments do pertain more aptly
unto him ; wherefore he weareth the more.

5. The Dalmatic ought to have two scarlet
orfreys [1] reaching all its length from top to

[1] So S. Isidore, in the place last referred to. He calls the
Dalmatic a ‘sacerdotal Vestment with purple stripes’ (‘tunica
sacerdotalis candida cum clauis ex purpura’). At present the
Dalmatic is usually crossed also behind by two transverse
stripes at top and bottom, to distinguish it from the Subdeacon’s Tunicle, which has only one, at the top. It has
also tassels hanging from the meeting-points of these stripes at

bottom back and fore, that the Bishop may shew himself to have, both in weal and woe, fervent charity unto God and his neighbour ; and this agreeth unto the commandment of both the Old and the New Testament, to wit, THOU SHALT LOVE THE LORD THY GOD WITH ALL THINE HEART, AND THY NEIGHBOUR AS THYSELF.[1] Thus also John,[2] BELOVED, NO NEW COMMANDMENT WRITE I UNTO YOU, BUT AN OLD COMMANDMENT, WHICH YE HAD FROM THE BEGINNING ; and again, A NEW COMMANDMENT I WRITE UNTO YOU. And sometimes the purple stripes be significant of faith in the Blood of Christ, so necessary unto either people. Upon the left side the Dalmatic is wont to have a fringe, for emblem of the cares of the active life, which the Bishop must have for his flock, agreeably unto the word of the Apostle,[3] which saith, BESIDE THOSE THINGS THAT ARE WITHOUT, THAT WHICH COMETH UPON ME DAILY, THE CARE OF ALL THE CHURCHES. The right side, lacking the fringe, is a token of the contemplation of heavenly

the back, supposed to be a survival of strings or laces by which the mouth of the Dalmatic was anciently opened to admit the head, and then drawn tight again.

[1] S. Luke x. 27.   [2] 1 S. John ii. 7, 8.

[3] 2 Cor. xi. 28.

things, which lacketh care, and is unmolested by the multitude of troubles.

6. Furthermore, certain Dalmatics have fringes fifteen-fold before and behind, because fifteen psalms [1] in the Old Testament, like fifteen branches or steps, do issue forth from the path of charity, and fifteen likewise in the New Testament do grow out of her work : to wit, CHARITY SUFFERETH LONG, CHARITY IS KIND, and so forth unto the words CHARITY NEVER FAILETH.[2]   But others have a fringe of twenty-eight before, and as many behind ; wherein the sevenfold Spirit is represented eight times over, Who filleth eight orders of them that praise God, that is, KINGS AND PEOPLE, PRINCES AND JUDGES, YOUNG MEN AND MAIDENS, OLD MEN AND CHILDREN.[3] Again, in the Dalmatic is diversity without division, because divers works of religion are done in the sight of God, yet in prayer is no difference at all.   And at the sides it is open beneath the armpits, putting him who weareth it in mind to follow in Christ's steps, Who was stabbed in the side with a spear.

7. Moreover, the Dalmatic maketh the form

---

[1] Pss. cxx.–cxxxiv.   [2] 1 Cor. xiii. 4-8.
[3] Ps. cxlviii. 11, 12.

of a cross, wherein it is a token of Christ's
Passion, and so is worn in the Office of the
Mass, in which that Passion is shown forth.   It
significth also holy religion, and mortification of
the flesh, and the spirit of supernal things.   If
white, it standeth for a holy and spotless life;
if red, for a martyr; but the white Dalmatic
wrought about with divers colours denoteth
purity together with the variety of virtues, and
is adorned with an orfrey, as it is written, AT
THY RIGHT HAND DID STAND THE QUEEN IN
A VESTURE OF GOLD, WROUGHT ABOUT WITH
DIVERS COLOURS.[1]

8. As touching that which agreeth unto the
Head, which is Christ, the Dalmatic by its
breadth and largeness is significant of His
mercy, which Himself more than all others
both taught and used; BE YE MERCIFUL, said
He, EVEN AS YOUR FATHER IS MERCIFUL.[2]
And BLESSED ARE THE MERCIFUL, FOR THEY
SHALL OBTAIN MERCY.[3]   He is that Samaritan,
our Neighbour, Who wrought mercifully with
us, pouring into our wounds wine and oil[4]:
THROUGH THE TENDER MERCY OF OUR GOD
THE DAYSPRING FROM ON HIGH HATH VISITED

[1] Ps. xlv. 10.   [2] S. Luke vi. 36.
[3] S. Matth. v. 7.   [4] S. Luke x. 34.

US[1]; NOT BY WORKS OF RIGHTEOUSNESS
WHICH WE HAVE DONE, BUT ACCORDING TO
HIS MERCY HE SAVED US,[2] coming for sinners'
sakes, that He might grant them pardon for
their sins ; Who said, I WILL HAVE MERCY AND
NOT SACRIFICE.[3]

We read in a Canon of Gregory[4] that in
the primitive Church neither Bishops nor
Deacons might wear the Dalmatic, save by
special licence of the Apostolic see.

9. The Deacons leave off their Dalmatics[5]
at the time of our Lord's Advent. For when
some measure of the splendour of holy service
is laid aside for a time, it seemeth to the minds
of the faithful to shine out the more brightly

---

[1] S. Luke i. 78.   [2] Tit. iii. 5.   [3] S. Matth. ix. 13.
[4] Grat. *Decret*. I. Dist. xxiii. c. x. ' Communis.'
[5] In the Roman rite the Deacon and Subdeacon leave off
their Dalmatic and Tunicle respectively on Fast-days (except
the Vigils of Saints' Days) ; on all days of Advent and Lent ;
on the Vigil of Pentecost before Mass (but not on Gaudete and
Laetare Sundays, nor on Christmas Eve, Holy Saturday at the
Blessing of the Candle and at Mass, nor on the Pentecostal
Ember Days) ; also at the Blessing of Candles and Procession
upon the Purification of Our Lady, at the Blessing of Ashes
and of Palms, and at the Procession of Palms. At these times,
in Cathedrals and principal Churches, they substitute the Folded-
Chasuble, a Vestment which they take off before the Gospel
and Epistle respectively, the Deacon folding it over his left
shoulder, and the Subdeacon ministering in his Albe. But in
inferior Churches, at these times, they minister in Albes alone.

when it is resumed, and is taken again with the more gladness ; because the more uncommon a thing is, the more we weary after it.[1]   Another reason wherefore the Deacon weareth not his Dalmatic in Advent, nor the Subdeacon his Tunicle, is this : that the Law (for which the Subdeacon standeth) did lack the beauty of the Gospel, and the Gospel's charity (which the Deacon signifieth) was not yet made manifest, before the Incarnation of the Lord.   Or it is for this, if thou wilt, that He Who should put upon us the robe of innocence and immortality was not yet come ; wherefore at this time the Vestments of gladness be laid aside.   Yet Chasubles are worn in Advent ; whereof somewhat hath been said by me in another book of the ' Rationale.'[2]   Nevertheless upon the Fasts in the Octave of Pentecost,[3] the Deacon may wear his Dalmatic.

[1] Grat. *Deer.* I. Dist. xcviii. c. 24, ' Legimus ' *ad finem.* A maxim whose truth must have been felt by all who have much to do with the Service of the Altar.

[2] ' Upon Fasts the Deacon hath a Chasuble folded over his left shoulder, because whatever labour we undergo in this life is borne in a figure upon that part ; until from the Left we pass over unto the Right, wherein we have our rest.'   *Kal.* ii. ' De Diacono.'

[3] *I.e.* the Ember Days.

CHAPTER XII

OF THE GLOVES

1. Oₗ the Gloves and their meaning.—2. Why the hands be
sometimes covered with Gloves, and sometimes bare of
them.—3. Further meanings of the Gloves ; and as touching
Christ.—4. Why the Gloves be made of the skins of kids.

1. BECAUSE by vain men-pleasing full many
spoil the good works they do ; immediately after
the Dalmatic put on, the Bishop according unto
the Apostolic rite covereth his hands with the
Gloves,[1] that his left hand may not know what
his right hand doeth.[2]   For by the Glove is
meetly figured caution, which doeth her work
before the eyes of men, yet hideth her plans in
secret none the less.   For albeit the Lord said,
LET YOUR LIGHT SO SHINE BEFORE MEN,

[1] But formerly they were the common property of both
Bishops and Priests.   The first extant mention of them as an
ecclesiastical Vestment is in the twelfth century, by Honorius
Augustodunensis, (died c. A.D. 1152).   They were often very
ornate.   Bp. Riculfus in his well-known Will (c. A.D. 915)
mentions 'annulum aureum unum cum gemmis pretiosis, et
vuantos (gants, gloves) paria unum ' (Patrol. cxxxii. 468).

[2] S. Matth. vi. 3.

THAT THEY MAY SEE YOUR GOOD WORKS,
AND GLORIFY YOUR FATHER WHICH IS IN
HEAVEN,[1] in type whereof the Glove hath a
golden circlet upon it ; yet the same Lord gave
this precept, TAKE HEED THAT YE DO NOT
YOUR ALMS BEFORE MEN, TO BE SEEN OF
THEM ; OTHERWISE YE HAVE NO REWARD OF
YOUR FATHER WHICH IS IN HEAVEN.[2]

2. Wherefore the hands be sometimes
covered with the Gloves, and sometimes bared,
because good works be sometimes hidden for
the avoiding of vainglory, and sometimes made
manifest to the edification of his neighbour.

3. They are without seam, for the actions of
the Bishop ought to be in right agreement with
his faith. As worn upon the hands, also, they
are a type of the examples of the Saints, which
are to be held fast by him in all his works ;
which works must be cleansed from all pollu-
tion, lest the LITTLE LEAVEN LEAVEN THE
WHOLE LUMP.[3] And by the Gloves themselves,
as being white,[4] we understand chastity and
purity, that his hands, that is, his works, may
be clean, and innocent of all stain.

[1] S. Matth. v. 16.   [2] *Ibid.* vi. 1.   [3] Gal. v. 9.
[4] Like most other Vestments, it appears that the Gloves
were originally white. But they were ornamented with jewels
from an early date.

4. As touching that which agreeth unto the Head, even Christ, the Gloves are made of the skins of kids, such as Rebekah put on the hands of Jacob, that their hairiness might set forth the likeness of his elder brother. And the skin of the kid is the likeness of sin, with which likeness Mother Rebekah—that is, the grace of the Holy Spirit—did array the hands of the true Jacob,[1] that is, the works of Christ ; to the end that He, the Second Adam, might bear the likeness of the elder, that is, the first Adam. For Christ did without sin take upon Himself the likeness of sin, that the mystery of the Incarnation might be concealed from the devil[2] ; and did hunger and thirst, suffered and was affrighted, slept and toiled, after the similitude of sinners. Unto Whom when He had FASTED FORTY DAYS AND FORTY NIGHTS, AND WAS AFTER-WARD AN HUNGRED,[3] the devil came in the likeness of the first Adam, and did essay to tempt Him ; yet he who had after the same manner conquered the first, was by the Second vanquisht.

---

[1] Gen. xxvii. 16.

[2] Not a theological dogma, but a poetical and mystic con-ceit ; and to be taken as such.

[3] S. Matth. iv. 2.

CHAPTER XIII

OF THE MITRE

1. Of the Bishop's Mitre, and of the Pope's Crown.—2. Of the two Horns of the Mitre.—3. Of the two Bands of the Mitre.—4. Of the Golden Circlet, the loftiness, and the Bands of the Mitre.—5. Further meanings of the Mitre; and as touching them that wear it.—6, 7. Of the Simple Mitre, and of the Orfreyed; and when they be severally worn.—8. Of the Regnum.—9, 10, 11. When the Bishop weareth the Mitre, and when he putteth it off, at the Holy Mass; and the reasons alleged by some.

1. HAVING put on the Chasuble, the Bishop placeth on his head the Mitre,[1] in the stead of the ancient Mitre or priestly bonnet; according unto the words, THOU HAST CROWNED HIM,

---

[1] This was always a peculiar ornament of Bishops. For the first six centuries the Mitre was, in Pelliccia's opinion, a simple linen fillet or cap, which began to grow ornate in the time of John of Cappadocia. The word *Mitra* originally denoted the headgear of an Asiatic woman; and in early times the *mitella* was worn by Christian women as a badge of virginity. The early Episcopal Mitre was called *mitta*, or *infula*, a fillet. When its use became distinctively ceremonial, it came to be called a Crown, and was regarded as strongly symbolical of the Episcopate, Bishops taking oath ' per coronam meam.'

O LORD, WITH GLORY AND HONOUR.[1] The Lord Pope hath moreover the Crown, the Imperial Tiara and Pall, the Purple Cloak and Blue Tunic, according to the Donation of Constantine, Emperor.[2]

2. Now the Mitre betokeneth the knowledge of both Testaments; for its two horns[3] are these same, the fore horn the New, the after horn the Old ; and both these the Bishop ought to know by heart,[4] and with them, as with a twofold

[1] Ps. viii. 5.

[2] 'Beato Siluestro . . . . et omnibus eius successoribus Pontificibus . . . . de praesenti contradimus . . . . diadema, uidelicet coronam capitis nostri, simulque frigium, necnon et superhumerale, uidelicet lorum, quod imperiale circumdare assolet collum ; uerum etiam clamidem purpuream, atque tunicam coccineam, et omnia imperialia indumenta.' [' To Blessed Silvester and all his successors in the Holy See we donate from this present the Diadem, to wit the Crown of our head, the Tiara, the Imperial Pall which is wont to surround the imperial neck, the purple cloak, the scarlet tunic, and all the Imperial robes.'] Donation of Constantine, Grat. *Decret.* I. Dist. xcvi. c. xiv. 'Constantinus.' The Frigium, or Phrygium, was so called because the Emperor's tiara was ' opere contexta Phrygio' (Du Cange, *sub voce*). (The reader will understand that I am not concerned to discuss the *genuineness* of the Donation of Constantine.)

[3] The Mitre was originally single in form, the division into two horns having come into general vogue about the tenth century.

[4] This in the ' Dark Ages,' when the Bible is popularly supposed to have been a sealed or unknown book ! We are very proud of our days of an ' Open Bible ' ; but if we read, marked, learned, and inwardly digested it as much as we talk about it, our national humility, learning, and piety might be materially increased.

horn, to smite the enemies of the Faith. Thus
ought he to appear horned unto his flock, as did
Moses in the eyes of Aaron and of the children
of Israel from his companying with the Word
of God, when bearing the two Tables of the Testimony he came down from Mount Sinai [1]; as
it is said in the thirty-fourth chapter of Exodus.
Yet do certain heretics condemn the Mitre with
its horns, and the Bishop wearing it ; who allege
unto the fostering of their error the words of
John in the Apocalypse,[2] I BEHELD ANOTHER
BEAST COMING UP OUT OF THE EARTH, AND
HE HAD TWO HORNS LIKE A LAMB, AND HE
SPAKE AS A DRAGON.

3. The two fringed bands [3] that hang from
behind the Mitre are the spirit and the letter ;
by which bands, or little tongues, it is set forth
that the Bishop ought to be ready both in the
mystical and in the historical interpretation of

[1] Ex. xxxiv. 29, 30. In E. V. we read, 'the skin of his
face shone.' But the Hebrew verb *káran*, to shine, is connected with *keren*, a horn ; and hence we have the verb
rendered ' horned ' in Aquila's version and in the Vulg. The
latter reads ' et ignorabat quod cornuta esset facies sua ex con-
sortio sermonis Domini.' Thus it comes to pass that so many
representations of Moses are horned.

[2] Rev. xiii. 11. The wresting of the Apocalypse to pur-
poses of this sort was plainly not unknown before the Refor-
mation ; cf. Proeme, § 14.

[3] *Fimbriae.* Called also *infulae.*

Holy Scripture. At their ends are fringes of red, denoting that he is prepared to defend the Faith and the Holy Scriptures, yea, even unto blood. And these hang down over his shoulders, in token that he should shew forth in his deeds that which he preacheth with his lips ; for that there is no part more eminent than the shoulders for might to labour, or for bearing of burthens ; wherefore by them works be meetly understood.

4. The golden circlet which embraceth the after and fore parts of the Mitre, sheweth that EVERY SCRIBE WHICH IS INSTRUCTED UNTO THE KINGDOM OF HEAVEN IS LIKE UNTO AN HOUSEHOLDER WHICH BRINGETH FORTH OUT OF HIS TREASURES THINGS NEW AND OLD.[1] Let the Bishop therefore take earnest heed that he desire not to be a master or ever he know how to be a disciple, lest if the BLIND LEAD THE BLIND, THEY BOTH FALL INTO THE DITCH[2] ; for it is written in the Prophet, BECAUSE THOU HAST REJECTED KNOWLEDGE, I WILL ALSO REJECT THEE, THAT THOU SHALT BE NO PRIEST TO ME.[3] Moreover, it well befitteth that the Mitre, whose shape goeth up into an

---

[1] S. Matth. xiii. 52. This, and much else of the Mitre hitherto, is to be found almost word for word in Innocent III.
[2] *Ibid.* xv. 14.   [3] Hos. iv. 6.

height,[1] should stand for the loftiness of wisdom, for the Bishop ought so to excel in knowledge those who are subject unto him, that in their relation to him they may worthily be called his flock.

The two bands which hang from the hinder part of the Mitre denote a twofold mindfulness. The former is the mindfulness of the Divine acts ; lest in celebrating he make little reckoning thereof, and be punished : and for a like reason even in the Old Testament he that would offer sacrifice was wont to walk amid the sound of bells, that thereby he might be received as worthy or be rejected as unworthy, by the Angel who was placed to guard the Temple. And the second band is the mindfulness of his sins, that he have contrition of them.

5. The Mitre, being sometimes of white linen, signifieth the whiteness and cleanness of Chastity ; wherefore this Vestment is very necessary unto the head, in which the body's five senses have their seat of life [2] ; for Chastity is easily violated, if thou corrupt these.

Also there be some who affirm that the

---

[1] The Mitre seems to have gradually grown in height, from its low stature at the beginning, to its present towering form.

[2] *Vigent.* Durandus's physiology is unimpeachable here, as regards the reflex action of physical sensations.

Bishop's Mitre is a type of the Crown of Thorns. And hence it cometh that in the Office of the Mass, wherein the Bishop representeth Christ in His Passion, it is the Deacon who putteth him the Mitre on and off; for that it is the Deacon's office to read the Gospel, in the which it is written concerning Christ crowned with thorns. And the two horns are the two precepts of Charity ; wherefore the Bishop taketh the Mitre in understanding that he ought to guard his five senses against the allurements of the world, so as to keep the laws of the two Testaments ; and to fulfil the two precepts of Charity, that he may be counted worthy to receive an eternal crown.

But the others, Priests and clergy, cover not in general their heads with any ornament,[1]

[1] To do so was strictly forbidden before the thirteenth century. But Pope Innocent IV. (A.D. 1243) allowed the resident monks of Canterbury to wear the Almuce, a fur hood which covered the head and hung down to the shoulders, because they found themselves 'grauissimis morbis implicitos' through worshipping bareheaded. The present biretta, or more properly berretta, took its origin in an ordinary layman's cap in the sixteenth century. It is regarded as the official headgear of the clergy, and so is worn in Church. Many object to the biretta on the ground of its being 'Italian.' To which it may be answered—all honour to Italy for having evolved a vestment which for simplicity, convenience, and seemliness leaves little to be desired ! The objection raised by some that the use of

albeit upon Festivals they be vested in every
other part of the body. And this is in part
because our joy is not yet full, for we joy not in
the possession of things present, but in the hope
of things to come; and in part because we be
journeying unto that estate, wherein we shall
· behold God with open face.

6. Now the Orfreyed Mitre [1] is to be used
from Easter unto Advent and from the Lord's
Nativity unto Septuagesima, and upon all
Doubles, and upon Feasts having nine Lessons
throughout the year, save upon the Feast of the
Holy Innocents, as shall be said in the chapter
of the Colours [2]; and upon the Sundays of the
aforesaid seasons, and in general whenever
Gloria in Excelsis and *Te Deum* shall be said.
For when these are said upon Feasts, wherein
we have in mind generally or specially the
excellence of the Head or the joy of the mem-

the biretta involves 'unfaithfulness to the Church of England,'
speaks volumes for the conscience of the objectors, but little
for their sense of humour.

[1] There are now three kinds of Mitre. (i.) *Mitra Simplex,*
of plain white silk or linen. (ii.) *M. Aurifrigiata,* adorned
with orfreys of gold. (iii.) *M. Pretiosa,* richly embroidered
and adorned with gold and precious stones. *Caeremoniale
Episcoporum,* Lib. I. c. xvii. Durandus gives only the two
former.

[2] Ch. xviii. § 6, *q. v.*

bers, we do rightly use the Orfreyed Mitre;
for the brightness of gold and jewels representeth joy.   But upon Fasts it is not to be used,
as followeth, because these have been ordained
for the blotting-out of sins, which upon them are
to be brought to remembrance ; and therefore
nought is then to be wrought or worn which
signifieth joy, but rather all that may mark
affliction and humility.

7. At other times the Orfreyed Mitre is
ruled not to be used, but the Simple : namely,
from Advent unto the Nativity (save that the
Lord Pope weareth the 'Orfreyed upon Gaudete
Sunday) and from Septuagesima unto Easter
(save of the Pope upon Laetare[1] Sunday,
Maundy Thursday at Mass only, and Holy
Saturday at Mass).   Also upon Feasts of three
Lessons occurring within these seasons, upon
all Vigils whereon a Feast is kept, at the Four
Seasons,[2] and upon Rogation days (save that
the Lord Pope weareth the Orfreyed upon the

---

[1] Gaudete Sunday (the Third Sunday in Advent) is so
called because the Introit for that day begins 'Gaudete in
Domino semper'; and Laetare Sunday (the Fourth Sunday
in Lent) because its Introit begins ' Laetare Jerusalem.'   See
Ch. xviii. § 6.

[2] *I.e.* the Ember Days, which fall in the four seasons of the
year respectively.

Feast of St. Mark at Mass only); also in the
Offices of the departed.[1]

8. This also is to be noted, that the Bishop
of Rome weareth the Regnum,[2] that is, the
Imperial Crown, in token of Imperial sway, and
the Mitre in token of High Priesthood; but he
weareth the Mitre everywhere and always, yet

[1] The *Cæremoniale Episcoporum* says: 'The Bishop uses
the Precious Mitre on the greater Feasts, and generally
when *Te Deum* and *Gloria in Excelsis* are said. Nevertheless the Orfreyed Mitre may be used on these same Festivals, but rather for convenience than of necessity. The
Orfreyed Mitre is used from Advent Sunday until Christmas
Day, except upon Gaudete Sunday, when the Precious is used;
from Septuagesima until Wednesday in Holy Week inclusively, except Laetare Sunday; upon all Fasted Vigils, Ember
Days, and Rogation Days, and in Litanies and Processions of a
penitential nature; on Holy Innocents' Day, unless it fall on a
Sunday; in Offices having three Lessons, and at private Bene-
dictions and Consecrations. The Simple Mitre is used on
Good Friday, and at Offices and Masses for the Dead.' Thus it
will be seen that Durandus, roughly speaking, assigns to his
'Orfreyed Mitre' the present use of the Precious, and to his
'Simple' those of the present Orfreyed and Simple combined;
the Precious Mitre being evidently a subsequent evolution from
the old Orfreyed, and having thrown the two others, as it were,
each a step downward.

[2] *I.e.* the Papal Tiara, now a triple crown, called sometimes Frigium, the token of Temporal Power. It is usually
represented as worn first by S. Silvester (A.D. 315) as granted
to him by the Donation of Constantine (see p. 94, n. 2), and
Platina, *Vit. Pont.*, *sub Silvestro*). The second crown was
added, it is said, by Boniface VIII., in token of the union of
the Spiritual and Temporal Powers; and the third, by Urban V.

not everywhere and always the Regnum, because
Pontifical authority hath priority of Imperial
power, and is of more dignity and extent.[1]   For
the Priesthood took precedence of the Kinghood
amongst the people of God ; for Aaron the first
High Priest was before Saul the first King, and
Noe was before Nimrod, as it is written,[2] THE
BEGINNING OF THE KINGDOM OF NIMROD
WAS BABYLON ; but Noe BUILDED AN ALTAR
UNTO THE LORD, AND OFFERED BURNT
OFFERINGS ON THE ALTAR.[3]   Wherefore the
Lord Pope doth not wear the Regnum, save on
certain days and in certain places, nor anywhere
within the Church, but without it.

9. As touching that which agreeth unto the
Head, even Christ, the Bishop's Mitre be-
tokeneth that which the Prophet,[4] speaking
of the Son, saith unto the Father, THOU HAST
CROWNED HIM WITH GLORY AND HONOUR :
THOU MADEST HIM TO HAVE DOMINION OVER
THE WORKS OF THINE HANDS.   It is the Name
WHICH IS ABOVE EVERY NAME, THAT AT THE
NAME OF JESUS EVERY KNEE SHOULD BOW,
OF THINGS IN HEAVEN, AND THINGS IN
EARTH, AND THINGS UNDER THE EARTH.[5]

---

[1] So Innocent III.   [2] Gen. x. 10.   [3] *Ibid.* ix. 20.
[4] Ps. viii. 5, 6.   [5] Phil. ii. 9, 10.

For upon the golden plate[1] of the High Priest's Mitre was graven the Four-Lettered Name[2] of the Lord, whose mystery we shall set forth in the chapter of the Vestments of the Law.[3] Thus by the Christian Mitre we understand that supreme glorifying of the Head or Person of Christ, which by reason of His Godhead we owe unto His Manhood, even as His Footstool is adored by reason of His Feet; for it is written, FALL DOWN BEFORE HIS FOOTSTOOL, FOR HE IS HOLY.[4]

10. And mark that as Zachary, Pope,[5] hath said, the Bishop who goeth unto the Altar to pray, or assisteth at the Altar or uttereth prayers before God, layeth aside his Mitre and Staff; because the Apostle forbiddeth that men should pray in Church with covered head, that they may contemplate the glory of God with

---

[1] The Fathers say that S. James, Bishop of Jerusalem, and S. John were in the habit of wearing this Golden Plate.

[2] Ex. xxviii. 36–38.

[3] Ch. xix. § 16, and notes.

[4] Ps. xcix. 5.

[5] Grat. *Decret.* 'De Cons.' Dist. I. c. 57 : 'Nullus epi-scopus . . . presumat . . . uelato capite altari Dei assistere. . . . Si quis uero presumpserit, a sacro Corpore et Sanguine D. N. J. C. sit suspensus.' [Let no Bishop presume to assist at God's Altar with head covered. If any do so, he shall be suspended from Communion.] So Pope Zacharias decreed, Synod of Rome, A.D. 743.

open face.[1] But when he turneth himself unto
the people to preach to them, he taketh again
the symbol of his dread authority. In like
manner Moses also urged the people's cause
with God by prayer, but God's matter brought
he before the people with the sword.

11. Lastly be it noted, that some Bishops
do give solemn blessing in the Mass, and
incense the Altar, without the Mitre; but
others do wear it the while. The former are
prompted by this thought, that in their solemn
blessing they are vicegerents of God, and that
God in a mystery blesseth through their mean ;
as it is said in the sixth chapter of the Book of
Numbers,[2] THEY SHALL INVOKE MY NAME
UPON THE CHILDREN OF ISRAEL, AND I WILL
BLESS THEM. The incensing of the Altar, too,
signifieth prayers, as in the eighth chapter of
the Apocalypse we are told that THE SMOKE
OF THE INCENSE ASCENDED UP FROM THE
PRAYERS OF THE SAINTS.[3] As pleading, therefore, the cause of the folk with God in prayer,

---

[1] 1 Cor. xi. 4.   [2] Num. vi. 27.

[3] Rev. viii. 4 : 'Ascendit fumus incensorum de orationi-
bus sanctorum.' Greek, ἀνέβη ὁ καπνὸς ταῖς προσευχαῖς—which
E. V. renders 'ascended *with* the prayers of the Saints.' With
all deference to our author—who does but lightly touch upon
the matter here—we may say that the Incensing of the Altar is
more strictly a type of the application of the atoning merit of
Our Lord to material things. It is the *censer* that is the type

they say that the Bishop ought to do this with reverence, that is, with his Mitre put off.

The latter, on the other hand, are minded that blessing and incensing are not essential to the consecration of the Body of Christ, but have regard merely unto solemnity of function ; and therefore do they perform these rites vested in the Mitre, that they may be distinguished from simple Priests thereby. For though the Bishop beareth more part than the mere Priest in those matters which belong unto solemn function, as in Vestments and the like, yet not so in those which have regard unto the Consecration itself. Still doth this reason appear in a manner insufficient, for it would accord therewith never [1] to put off the Mitre at Mass, save when those words are pronounced at which the change of species taketh place.

of prayer ; the incense being the merits of Our Lord. As the censer conveys and offers on high the smoke of the incense, so our prayers convey and offer on high the merits of the one acceptable Sacrifice. In the Apocalypse (v. 8) we read of φιάλας χρυσᾶς γεμούσας θυμιαμάτων, αἵ εἰσιν αἱ προσευχαὶ τῶν ἁγίων—'golden vials full of odours, which [the vials, not the odours] are the prayers of the Saints.' The passage above quoted also illustrates this. We do not want types of things we have or can make for ourselves—and prayer is such a thing ; but only of things we have not, or have not always fully and completely.

[1] Some editors leave out this 'never' (non). I have retained it, as its omission seems to miss Durandus' whole point.

CHAPTER XIV

OF THE RING

1, 2. Of the Ring and its meaning, as a sign of plighted love. 3. Of the Ring as a seal ; and of the Finger, whereon it is worn.—4. Of the Ring as golden, and round.

1. THE Ring[1] is the sign of plighted faith, wherewith Christ hath espoused His Bride Holy Church, that she may have authority to say concerning herself, *The Lord Jesus Christ hath espoused me with His Ring, Whose watchmen and teachers are the Bishops and Prelates, who bear rings as a figure and token of this very thing*; those watchmen whereof saith the Spouse in the Canticles,[2] THE WATCHMEN THAT GO ABOUT THE CITY FOUND ME. This is the Ring that was given by the Father unto his son

[1] An integral part of the Episcopal ornaments from very early times. It is mentioned by S. Isidore of Seville in the sixth century. It is placed upon the right hand of the Bishop by the priest assistant, who first kisses the Ring and the Bishop's hand. The Ring has usually been large and massive, set with a jewel and adorned with devices.

[2] Cant. iii. 3.

returning, according to that of the Gospel,[1] PUT
A RING ON HIS HAND; and from this place of
the Gospel it is thought that the use of the
Ring hath been derived.

2. The Bishop's Ring therefore signifieth
the integrity of plighted troth, namely, that he
✓ should love the Church, God's Spouse, com-
mitted unto him, even as himself, and should
keep her pure and chaste for her Heavenly
Bridegroom; as in that of Paul,[2] I HAVE
ESPOUSED YOU TO ONE HUSBAND, THAT I
MAY PRESENT YOU AS A CHASTE VIRGIN TO
CHRIST; and that he may be mindful that he
himself is not a master, but a pastor. Of this
Bridegroom and Bride John Evangelist saith,[3]
HE THAT HATH THE BRIDE IS THE BRIDE-
GROOM; BUT THE FRIEND OF THE BRIDE-
GROOM, WHICH STANDETH AND HEARETH
HIM, REJOICETH GREATLY BECAUSE OF THE
BRIDEGROOM'S VOICE. The Bishop, therefore,
is the Vicar and Friend of the Bridegroom;
and being His Vicar, is himself also the Bride-
groom in certain wise.

3. Again, with a Ring of old they were wont
to seal letters; wherefore the Bishop weareth a

---

[1] S. Luke xv. 22.   [2] 2 Cor. xi. 2.
[3] S. John iii. 29.

Ring, for that he should seal up the mysteries of Scripture and the holy things of the Church from the faithless, and reveal them unto the humble.

And as touching that which agreeth unto the Head, even Christ, the Ring on the finger is a type of the gift of the Holy Ghost ; for the finger, which is a part jointed and distinct, giveth an hint of the Holy Ghost, according unto that scripture, THE MAGICIANS SAID, THIS IS THE FINGER OF GOD [1] ; and in another place, IF I WITH THE FINGER OF GOD CAST OUT DEVILS, BY WHOM DO YOUR SONS CAST THEM OUT? [2]

4. Also the Ring, being golden and round, √representeth the perfection of the Spirit's gifts, which Christ hath received without measure,[3] for that in Him dwelleth ALL THE FULNESS OF THE GODHEAD BODILY.[4] For HE THAT COMETH FROM HEAVEN IS ABOVE ALL,[5] unto Whom GOD GAVE NOT THE SPIRIT BY MEASURE, saying, UPON WHOM THOU SHALT SEE THE SPIRIT DESCENDING, AND REMAINING ON HIM, THE SAME IS HE THAT BAP-

[1] Ex. viii. 19.
[2] S. Luke xi. 19, 20.   The clauses are transposed.
[3] S. John iii. 34.   [4] Col. ii. 9.   [5] S. John iii. 31.

TISETH.[1] For THE SPIRIT OF WISDOM AND UNDERSTANDING SHALL REST UPON HIM.[2] And He of His fulness distributeth in divers gifts, giving unto one, as saith the Apostle, THE WORD OF KNOWLEDGE, TO ANOTHER THE GIFT OF HEALING, TO ANOTHER THE WORKING OF MIRACLES,[3] and so forth; and this the visible Bishop imitateth, making in the Church some Priests, some Deacons, others Subdeacons, and the rest. Wherefore it is not amiss that the jewelled Ring gleameth upon the finger of the Bishop; for by Him, of Whom it is the mystic symbol, are given the bright gifts of grace.

---

[1] S. John i. 33.   [2] Is. xi. 2.   [3] I Cor. xii. 9, 10.

CHAPTER XV

OF THE PASTORAL STAFF

1. Of the Pastoral Staff, its origin and meaning.—2. Of the Names and Meanings thereof.—3. Of the Material and Shape of the Staff, and wherefore it is so.—4. Of the three Functions of the Staff, as set forth by its three parts.—5. Of the historical reason wherefore the Pope useth not the Staff.—6. Of the mystical reason wherefore the Pope useth not the Staff.—7. Of the Pastoral Staff as touching Christ.

1. THE Pastoral Staff[1] signifieth Pastoral Correction, according unto that which is said by the Consecrator unto him that is consecrated, '*Receive the Staff of the Pastoral Office, that in the chastising of vices thou mayest be*

---

[1] This, the sceptre of spiritual authority, has many names; it is called *virga, cambutta, sambuca, pedum, crocia,* and *ferula.* Its use may be traced at least as far as the sixth century (S. Greg. Tur. *De Mirac. S. Mart.* L. i. c. 4). And tradition carries it back to the time of S. Peter himself. The essential notion of it is threefold—it may be called a Crook, a Sceptre, and a Rod; in other words, it expresses the threefold function of the Prelate, as a Shepherd, to gather in the wanderers to the true Fold; a King, to rule his spiritual subjects, under Christ; and a Master, to correct the froward and spur on the indolent. Baronius (*c.* A.D. 504) says that the Pastoral Staff was used by Bishops as early as the fourth century.

angry, and sin not.[1] And hereof also the Apostle,[2] SHALL I COME TO YOU WITH A ROD? By the Pastoral Staff therefore we do understand the priestly power, which Christ did confer upon His Apostles, when sending them out to preach He charged them that they should bear staves. And Moses also was sent into Egypt with a rod.

2. Thus the Staff is derived from both the Law and the Gospel, being called both the Pastoral Staff, and the Crosier, and the Crook, and the Rod. For Moses had a Rod by the commandment of God, which wrought terrible things in sea and sky, bringing food from heaven, and water from the rock; and drave his flock unto the LAND FLOWING WITH MILK AND HONEY.[3] Further, the Staff is Doctrinal Authority. For by it the weak are sustained, the restless rallied, and the erring drawn to repentance; whence it is called Pedum, the Crook, which is the name of the curved wooden staff wherewith shepherds draw back their herds by the feet.

---

[1] The *Pontifical* has these words :—'Accipe baculum pastoralis officii, ut sis in corrigendis uitiis pie saeviens, iudicium sine ira tenens, in fouendis uirtutibus auditorum animos demulcens, in tranquillitate seueritatis censuram non deserens.'

[2] 1 Cor. iv. 21.   [3] Josh. v. 6.

3. Now the Staff is for the most part made of ivory and wood,[1] which are joined together by a knop[2] of crystal and gilt; the ivory above is crooked, and the wood below hath an iron point, but not much of the end is hidden therein.[3] The ivory is the severity of the Law, the wood the Gospel's gentleness; and these twain are joined with the knop, as it were by the Divinity of Jesus Christ. Or, if thou wilt, the ivory is the Bishop's severity, and the wood his gentleness, both the which in his judgments he combineth with the BOND OF CHARITY; for either sternness or mildness lacketh exceedingly, if the one be held to without the other; and to this end the iron is blunt, for that justice is tempered with mercy. The Staff is crooked,

[1] So always in primitive times; generally either of elder (hence probably the name *sambuca*, 'sambucus' meaning elder) or of cypress. Martigny says most commonly the latter (*Dict. des Antiq. Chrét.* s.v. 'Évêques').

[2] These developed into most elaborate pieces of tabernacle-work, like the knops of chalices, octagonal, and adorned with images set with precious stones. In Dugdale's *Monasticon* the following is quoted from an inventory of Lichfield Cathedral: 'Imprimis, a head of a Bishop's Staff of silver and gilt, with one knop and pearls, and other stones, having an image of our Saviour on the one side, and an image of S. John Baptist on the other, weighing eighteen ounces.' Visitors to Oxford are familiar with the exquisite Pastoral Staves preserved at New, Corpus Christi, and S. John's.

[3] 'Modice tamen reconditur.'

to signify the recalling of the contrite into penance. Sometimes the curve maketh the shape of an head, because eternal life is promised unto them that turn to God; and sometimes round the curved part is written,

CVM . IRATVS . FVERIS . MISERICORDIAE . RECORDABERIS,

which is, being interpreted, *In wrath remember mercy* [1]; lest by reason of the backslidings of his flock the shepherd's wrath should becloud the eyes of his reason. Sometimes upon the knop is inscribed HOMO, that the Bishop may remember himself to be but man, nor be puffed up with the power committed unto him; sometimes also hard by the point is written PARCE, that in his discipline he may spare those subject unto him, and being merciful may for his mercy obtain mercy.

4. The Staff is sharp at the end, straight in the midst, and crooked at the top; this meaneth that the Bishop ought to goad on the idle, to direct the feeble with his own rightness, and to gather the wanderers together; hence the verse,

COLLIGE . SVSTENTA . STIMVLA . VAGA . MORBIDA . LENTA,

---

[1] Hab. iii. 2.

I

which being interpreted is,

> Gather, and guide, and goad unto the goal
> The stray, the ailing, and the tarrying soul ;

wherein if thou refer word to his word, thou wilt find that all the foregoing are contained.   Or it may be thus,

> ATTRAHE . PER . PRIMVM . MEDIO . REGE .
> PVNGE . PER . IMVM,

which is

> The Top, to draw into the road :
> The Midst, to rule : the End, to goad.[1]

5. But the Bishop of Rome useth not the Pastoral Staff, partly for an historical, and in part for a mystical reason.   The historical reason is as follows.   The Blessed Apostle Peter sent Martial his disciple (whom the Lord made to be His follower when He said, EXCEPT YE BECOME AS THIS LITTLE CHILD, YE SHALL NOT ENTER INTO THE KINGDOM OF HEAVEN [2]) with certain others to preach unto the Germans.   When they had gone a twenty-days' journey, Martial's col-

---

[1] The full quatrain is thus :

> In Baculi forma, Praesul, datur haec tibi norma :
> Attrahe per curuum, medio rege, punge per imum ;
> Attrahe peccantes, rege iustos, punge uagantes ;
> Attrabe, sustenta, stimula—uaga, morbida, lenta.

[2] S. Matth. xviii. 3, 4.

league, Frontus, died, and Martial returned to
tell this to Peter; whereupon Peter said unto
him, 'Take this Staff and touch him with it,
and say, *In the Name of the Lord arise and
preach.*' This Martial did, touching him on the
fortieth day after his death; and he arose, and did
preach. And it was thus that Saint Peter.put
away his Staff from him and gave it unto his
flock; nor did he recover it again. But on the
other hand, Innocent the Third, Pope, wrote in
the *Speculum Ecclesiae* that Blessed Peter sent
his Staff unto Eucherius,[1] first Bishop of Trèves,
whom he appointed, together with Valerius
and Maternus, to preach the Gospel unto the
Teutonic people; and to him Maternus suc-
ceeded as Bishop, who had been raised up from
death by Peter's Staff.[2] And this Staff is
preserved by the Church of Trèves with great
veneration even unto this day[3]; wherefore the

[1] *Cir.* A.D. 362. In the legend of Maternus, Bishop of
Cologne, the see of Trèves is said to have been founded in the
first century, and Maternus, Eucherius, and Valerius were its
first Bishops.—Greg. Tur. *Vit. Pat.* c. 17, § 4, p. 1237.

[2] This variant of the story is also given by S. Thomas
Aquinas, *In IV. Sententiarum*, Distinct. xxiv. Qu. 3; and by
Honorius of Autun, and Peter of Clugni.

[3] Georgius says that Egbert, Archbishop of Trèves, A.D. 980,
obtained this Staff from Werinus, Archbishop of Cologne,
whither a former Bishop, Bruno, had transferred it. The Case
in which the Staff is contained preserves the above history, in a

Pope useth the Staff in that diocese, and none other.[1]

6. But the mystical reason is this, that the drawing-in of wanderers, as symbolised by the crookedness of the top of the Staff, is not needed in the case of the Bishop of Rome ; for that none can altogether turn away from him.[2] Moreover the Staff is a type of that constraining power, which the other Bishops receive at the hands of men, and therefore do they receive and hold their Staves from those set over them. But the Pope, because he receiveth his power from God alone, hath not the Staff.

7. Lastly, as touching that which agreeth unto the Head, even Christ, the Bishop's Staff

very ancient inscription. This case is covered with plates of silver, curiously gilt, and adorned with jewels ; and round the knop of the Staff are small images of the Twelve Apostles. See Pugin's *Glossary*, under ' Pope.'

[1] The last-quoted authority questions whether the Popes did not at one time carry a Pastoral Staff, and cites from the ceremonies of the election of Pope Pascal II. (A.D. 1099) a statement to the effect that ' a Staff was given into his hand.'

[2] As wielder of a jurisdiction extending to all the baptised. S. Thomas Aquinas makes the curvature of the Pastoral Staff denote a limited jurisdiction. The Triple Cross may be said to have taken its place as a Papal emblem. It is, however, an open question whether the Popes ever used the Pastoral Staff. There are three distinct ancient representations of S. Gregory with one ; and the tendency to deny its use by the early Popes seems to date from the twelfth century.

signifieth the power of Christ, whereof the
Psalmist saith, THE ROD OF THY KINGDOM IS
A RIGHT SCEPTRE, that is, a sceptre of direction,
FOR THOU HAST LOVED RIGHTEOUSNESS, AND
HATED INIQUITY[1]; and elsewhere, THOU SHALT
RULE THEM WITH A ROD OF IRON.[2] The hard-
ness of the iron signifieth the might of right-
ness, with which Christ SHALL BREAK THE
UNRIGHTEOUS IN PIECES LIKE A POTTER'S
VESSEL.[3]

Yet is the power of Christ not the power of
the rod alone, but the power also of the Staff,
for it doth not only chasten, but sustaineth;
whence the Psalmist,[4] THY ROD AND THY STAFF
COMFORT ME.

---

[1] Ps. xlv. 7, 8.
[2] *Ibid.* ii. 9.   Vulg. *reges*; E.V. 'thou shalt bruise.'
[3] *Ibid.*   [4] *Ibid.* xxiii. 4.

CHAPTER XVI

OF THE SUDARIUM

1. Of the use of the Sudarium, and of the meaning thereof.
2. Of its signification as touching ourselves.

1. AND now, having done with the Nine Vestments peculiar to the Bishop, let us for a space consider certain others : whereof the first shall be the Sudarium.   This is a linen cloth, which he that serveth the Bishop hath alway ready, wherewith the latter may wipe away from himself all the sweat and unnecessary moistness of the body ; and it signifieth the care we must have to wipe away all this life's human defilements through the examples of the holy Fathers, by the which we are confirmed unto patience.   For as sweat in the body, so is that weariness in the soul, whensoever it doth bedew as it were the brow of the conscience through the consciousness of sin.

2. Let us have, then, as it were a Napkin of linen, chastened and cleansed by many blows,

with which to wipe off the affections of this world; and with David[1] and Job[2] laying aside sadness, let us wipe away all that may oppress us.

In some Churches the Deacon hath a Sudarium, and layeth it down on the right side of the Altar, that if aught foul should chance to come near he may wipe it away, and so may keep the Priest's Sudarium clean every whit.

The meaning of the Sudarium is almost the same as that of the Maniple; whereof I have spoken above.

[1] 2 Sam. xii. 20.   [2] Job xlii.

CHAPTER XVII

OF THE PALL

1. Of the Pall and its origin.—2. Of the high rank of them that wear the same.—3. Of the Form, Material, and Fashioning thereof.—4. Of the circular part of the Pall, and of the meaning thereof. —5. Of the two Strips of the Pall, and what they signify.—6, 7. Of the Pall as double on the left side.—8. Of the four Crosses on the Pall, and of the meaning thereof.—9, 10. Of the three Pins fastened in the Pall, and their meaning.—11, 12. Of the use of the Pall as touching Times and Places.—13. Of the days and seasons wherein the Pall shall be worn.—14. Of the Palls of the Popes.

1. NOW in due course we shall subjoin somewhat concerning the Pall.[1] This Vestment per-

[1] The Pall, the emblem of full jurisdiction in the Bishop, was, according to Gregory Nazianzen, originally an ornament of the heathen emperors in the character of Pontifex Maximus, and was first presented by Constantine the Great to the Bishop of Jerusalem. But from very early times there was a large woollen Vestment worn by Bishops generally, properly called ὠμοφόριον, and worn, according to Liberatus, by S. Mark, at Alexandria. This Vestment, which Isidore of Pelusium says was a figure of the lost sheep borne on the shoulders of the Good Shepherd, was, according to Pelliccia and others, the prototype of the Pallium ; having been gradually cut down, until only its outer edges remained. After a time it acquired a jurisdictional meaning, and Emperors and Patriarchs began to bestow it upon

taineth unto Patriarchs, Primates, and Metropolitans, to distinguish them from the rest of the Bishops, for that unto these is committed a special dignity of privilege ; wherefore I have in no wise mentioned it under the heads of the foregoing Vestments common or peculiar.

In the Pall, then, we find at once both the Ephod and the Breastplate of the Priest in the Law. For it may be called Superhumeral, in that it falleth over both the Bishop's shoulders, and Rationale or Breastplate, in that it falleth thence upon his breast, and is fastened there ; for the ancient High Priest had both Ephod and Breastplate joined together by chains of gold. Some there be, however, who hold that the Breastplate hath to-day no Vestment to represent it ; concerning which matter I will speak in the last chapter of this Book.[1] Others say that the Pall was instituted in the stead of the Golden Plate; though it seem more

chief Bishops; then the right of conferring it passed by degrees into the hands of the Roman Pontiff, and it became customary in the Roman Church for Metropolitans to go to Rome to receive it ; until, at the Fourth Lateran Council (A.D. 1215), it was formally decreed that Oriental Patriarchs must receive the Pall from the Pope. And from that day to this its bestowal has been, in the Roman Catholic Church, an indispensable condition of the full exercise of Metropolitan authority.

[1] § 14.

likely that the Orfreyed Mitre representeth the Plate.

2. Now the Pall as worn by these greater ones signifieth the authority wherewith they ought to rule and restrain, not only those submitted unto them, but also themselves; for by this means is won that golden chain which those receive who strive lawfully, of which Solomon speaketh in the Proverbs,[1] saying, MY SON, HEAR THE INSTRUCTION OF THY FATHER, AND FORSAKE NOT THE LAW OF THY MOTHER: FOR THEY SHALL BE AN ORNAMENT OF GRACE UNTO THY HEAD, AND CHAINS ABOUT THY NECK. But even as the chain or prize was not wont to be given, save unto them that strove lawfully, according unto that word of the Apostle, MANY RUN, BUT ONE RECEIVETH THE PRIZE,[2] so also none shall make his way unto the honour of the Pall, save that he have first laboured lawfully in each degree of office ecclesiastical. For even as touching the offices of this world they confer not the highest place upon them that are but just entered upon the threshold of their labours, but upon such as have been approved in their passage through many degrees; and that degree excelleth the rest, where-

---

[1] Prov. i. 8, 9.   [2] 1 Cor. ix. 24.

unto more protracted labour and longer service have given the precedence.

· The Pall, then, is worn over all Vestments,[1] that the other Ministers when they see it may be exhorted unto lawful striving. And the Bishop, when he putteth it on and off,[2] doth kiss it, to show his own great desire of contending lawfully, and of deserving the prize.

3. It is woven of white wool,[3] having a

[1] 'When the Pall is put upon the Archbishop, it is always placed over the Chasuble, so that its double part shall lie on the left shoulder' (*Caer. Ep.* I. xvi. 'De Pallio').

[2] The following account of the putting-on of the Pall, when the Bishop celebrates High Mass, may be of interest :—' If the Bishop may wear the Pall, and it be convenient for him to do so upon that day, it is brought by a Subdeacon from the Altar, in both hands, covered with a veil. The Deacon then takes it and offers it to the Bishop, that he may kiss it upon the cross behind ; and he has a care, in holding it, to take the double part in his right hand, and the single in his left. And while he puts it on, the Subdeacon raises with his right hand the part which must hang down from the back, and they arrange it evenly over the Bishop's shoulders, so that the double part goes over his left shoulder. This done, the Deacon takes one of the three pins, which are brought by an Acolyth ; and the fairest of these he fixes into the front cross of the Pall, which is before the breast, and another into that on the left shoulder ; while the Subdeacon fixes the third into the cross behind ; and all are fixed in such a manner that they may go through the Cross, but not pierce the Pall nor touch the Chasuble, and that the jewels fixed to the pins may lie on the right-hand side of him that puts them in' (*Caer. Ep.* L. II. c. viii. 'De Missa Solemni Episcopo celebrante ').

[3] ' The office of making and keeping the Pallia belongs to the

circular part confining the shoulders, and two strips hanging down before and behind ; on the left it is double, on the right single ; and it hath four purple crosses, one before, one behind, one on the right, and one on the left ; there be also three pins fastened therein. Some things there be, which may not be done by the Metropolitan without the Pall, nor is it lawful to wear it save upon fixt days. And all these things are tinged

Subdeacons Apostolic, who prepare them of pure white wool in the following manner. The holy women of the Monastery of S. Agnes . . . offer yearly two white lambs on the Altar of that Church on S. Agnes' Day, while *Agnus Dei* is sung in the High Mass. These lambs are received by two Canons of the Church of S. John Lateran, and are afterwards consigned by them to the Subdeacons Apostolic, who send the lambs out to pasture till shearing-time. Their wool, and other wool mixed with it, is spun into yarn from which Pallia are woven of the breadth of three fingers, of a round form, to encircle the shoulders of Prelates. The Pallium has a band hanging down about a Roman foot long, and at the ends small leaden weights with boss · covered with black silk sewn on the bands, which hang down before and behind, and on each shoulder. The Pallia, thus prepared, are carried to the Church of S. Peter, and there placed by the Canons of that Church over the bodies of the Apostles Peter and Paul beneath the High Altar ; where, having kept vigil according to custom, they leave them all night, and then return them to the Subdeacons, who reserve them in a convenient place' (*Caer. Rom.* L. I. § 10; Pugin, *sub* ' Pall '). The form of granting the Pall in the *Pontifical* is :— 'Tradimus tibi Pallium de corpore B. Petri sumptum, in quo est plenitudo Pontificalis officii, cum Patriarchalis, uel Archiepiscopalis nominis appellatione,' &c. The form of the Pallium is yet to be found upon the Arms of the See of Canterbury.

with spiritual mysteries and big with heavenly
meaning, for as the Scripture witnesseth, THE
PARABLES OF KNOWLEDGE ARE IN THE TREA-
SURES OF WISDOM.[1] In the wool of the Pall we
see asperity ; in its whiteness, kindness : for the
Church's discipline useth towards the rebellious
and froward, severity, but gentleness towards
the contrite and humble. Wherefore the Pall
is made not of the wool of any and every
animal, but only of the sheep, which is a gentle
creature ; thus the Prophet[2] saith, HE WAS LED
AS A SHEEP TO THE SLAUGHTER, AND LIKE
A LAMB DUMB BEFORE HIS SHEARER, SO
OPENED HE NOT HIS MOUTH.   Hereunto
agreeth the word we are told concerning that
man half-dead with wounds, whom the Samaritan led into the inn and applied unto him wine
and oil,[3] that the wine might eat into his
wounds, and the oil foment them ; even so he
who hath the chief part in the healing of wounds
must apply the bite of severity, as wine, and
the gentleness of love, as it were oil.   Which
also is well shewn by the Ark of the Tabernacle,
wherein were contained, with the Tables, the
Rod and the Manna ; for in the mind of him

[1] Ecclus. i. 25.   [2] Is. liii. 7, as quoted Acts viii. 32.
[3] S. Luke x. 34.

that ruleth there ought to be, together with the knowledge of Scripture, both the Rod of guidance, and the Manna of kindness, that his severity be neither unduly severe, nor his love more indulgent than is meet. Again, the wool is of little price, whereof the Pail is made, that it may be precious not in itself, but in that which in itself it pourtrayeth, and may be meet to be looked upon, not with the eyes, but with the mind ; in understanding that it is worn for its meaning, rather than for its beauty.

4. The circular part of the Pall, which confineth the shoulders, is that fear of the Lord by which works are wrought, so as neither to decline unto lawlessness, nor relax unto excess. For discipline must restrain the left hand from that which is unlawful, through fear of punishment, while it tempereth the right hand from extravagance, by the love of right ; wherefore blessed is the man who feareth alway. For according to the word of Solomon,[1] THE FEAR OF THE LORD DRIVETH AWAY SIN ; BUT HE THAT LIVETH WITHOUT FEAR SHALL NOT BE JUSTIFIED. Wherefore this circle of the Pall doth confine the shoulders below 'he neck, to

---

[1] Not Solomon, but Ecclus. i. 21, 22.

denote that he who weareth it ought to be one
in word and deed.

5. The two strips, the one extending behind
the back and the other before the breast of the
Bishop, we hold to be a sign of the cares and
anxieties of this life ; which do too often on this
wise cumber and weigh down the heart and
shoulders of the Bishop, causing him to stoop
from that erectness which should be his, so that
he must bear in mind and body the burthen of
vain and transitory things. For this reason the
Pall is fitted on from right and left before and
behind, before the breast and over the shoulders,
this signifying, that casting such things behind
him [1] he shall often restore himself to himself.

Hereby are also signified the life active and
the life contemplative ; which the Prelate ought
to live in such wise, that after the example of
Moses he may now climb up into the Mount
and there hold parleyings of wisdom with the
Lord, and now may go down into the camp, to
take thought for the needs of his people. For
he must be very ready to have a care that
though he devote himself often unto others, he

---

[1] 'Ut his posthabitis in seipsum redire intelligatur.' The
play in the word ' posthabitis ' is necessarily impaired in translation. *Posthabeo* means ' to throw off, disregard, a thing.'

restore himself sometimes unto himself; being with Martha duly busied about his constant ministry, the while with Mary he hearkeneth unto the words of the Saviour. And by either strip he is weighed down, because THE CORRUPTIBLE BODY PRESSETH DOWN THE SOUL, AND THE EARTHLY TABERNACLE WEIGHETH DOWN THE MIND THAT MUSETH UPON MANY THINGS.[1]

6. The Pall is double on the left side, as was also the Breastplate, but single on the right. For this present life, which the left side signifieth, is subject unto many troubles, and we cannot be free from a double state therein; being now puffed up with well-being, now broken with adversity; now seeking the things of earth, now cleaving unto heavenly things; serving now the flesh, now the spirit. But the life to come, which is signified by the right side, is gathered up into one endless rest; as the Very Truth declareth, when He saith, MARTHA, MARTHA, THOU ART CAREFUL AND TROUBLED ABOUT MANY THINGS, BUT ONE THING IS NEEDFUL; AND MARY HATH CHOSEN THAT GOOD PART, WHICH SHALL NOT BE TAKEN AWAY FROM HER.[2]

7. Again, the Pall is double on the left side, that the Prelate may in his day be strong to

---

[1] Wisd. ix. 15.   [2] S. Luke x. 41, 42.

bear the troubles of this present life ; but single
on the right, that with his whole heart he may
sigh to win the tranquillity of the life to come.
Whereof the Psalmist,[1] ONE THING HAVE I
DESIRED OF THE LORD WHICH I WILL REQUIRE:
EVEN THAT I MAY DWELL IN THE HOUSE OF
THE LORD ALL THE DAYS OF MY LIFE, TO
BEHOLD THE FAIR BEAUTY OF THE LORD, AND
TO VISIT HIS TEMPLE. For There is neither
doubleness nor wrinkle, but prosperity without
adversity, and joy without sadness, and felicity
without grief.

8. The four purple crosses be the Four
Cardinal Virtues, to wit Justice, Fortitude, Tem-
perance, and Prudence ; and these do usurp the
name of virtue falsely unto themselves, nor lead
unto true blessing or glory, except they be made
purple in the Blood of Christ's Cross. Where-
fore the Lord said unto His Apostles, EXCEPT
YOUR RIGHTEOUSNESS SHALL EXCEED THE
RIGHTEOUSNESS OF THE SCRIBES AND PHARI-
SEES, YE SHALL IN NO CASE ENTER INTO
THE KINGDOM OF HEAVEN.[2] This is that
KING'S PURPLE DYED WITH STRIPES,[3] whereof

---

[1] Ps. xxvii. 4.　　　[2] S. Matth. v. 20.
[3] Cant. vii. 5. A difficult passage. Vulg. 'Cumae capitis
tui sicut purpura regis vincta canalibus.' A.V. 'the hair of

K

Solomon speaketh in the Song of Songs. He therefore that is adorned with the honour of the Pall, if he wish to be that which is exprest in the forepart, ought to have Justice, that he may render unto every man his own ; for the after part he ought to have Prudence, that he may beware of that which is harmful unto any ; for the left, Fortitude, that ills cast him not down ; and for the right, Temperance, that he be not puffed up with prosperity.

9. The three pins which are fastened in the Pall, one before the breast, one over the left shoulder, and one behind the back, are not made for piercing—that is to say, not for the piercings of this life—but to fasten the Pall and the Chasuble together ; and some little rings were fixt of old in the Chasuble, into which the pins were inserted, making both Pall and Chasuble fast, so that the former should not move out of his place. In these three pins we may discern Faith, Hope, and Charity, without which the Pall cannot fitly be had by the Bishop. They denote also compassion for his neighbour,

thine head is like purple ; the king is held (marg. *bound*) in the galleries.' R.V. 'the king is held captive in the tresses thereof.' Durandus gives ' purpura regis *tincta* canalibus,' which would doubtless bear the signification I have assigned in the text.

the administration of his office, and the discrimination of his judgment ; whereof the first
with sorrow, the second with labour, and the
third with fear, pricketh his soul. With the
first of these the Apostle was prickt, when he
said[1] WHO IS WEAK, AND I AM NOT WEAK?
WHO IS OFFENDED, AND I BURN NOT? and with
the second, when he said,[2] BESIDE THOSE
THINGS THAT ARE WITHOUT, THAT WHICH
COMETH UPON ME DAILY, THE CARE OF ALL
THE CHURCHES. With the third Job was prickt,
saying,[3] IF THE RIGHTEOUS SCARCELY BE SAVED,
WHERE SHALL THE UNGODLY AND THE SINNER
APPEAR?   Upon the right shoulder there is no
pin fastened, for that our everlasting rest hath
no prick of affliction nor sting of sorrow.   For
GOD SHALL WIPE AWAY ALL TEARS FROM THE
EYES OF THE SAINTS, AND AT THAT TIME
THERE SHALL BE NO MORE EITHER SORROW
OR CRYING, NEITHER SHALL THERE BE ANY
MORE PAIN; FOR THE FORMER THINGS ARE
PASSED AWAY.[4]

---

[1] 2 Cor. xi. 29.   [2] *Ibid.* 28.
[3] 1 S. Pet. iv. 18.   Any connection of these words with
Job, except in an imaginary point of view, is of course a
mistake. But there is something like it in Prov. xi. 31, 'Si
iustus in terra recipit, quanto magis impius et peccator?'
[4] Rev. xxi. 4.

10. The pins must be of gold, the end sharp, and the head round, with a precious stone set in it ; because of a truth the good pastor, in caring for his sheep, is afflicted on earth, but shall be crowned in Heaven ; where he shall have that precious pearl spoken of by the Lord in the Gospel,[1] THE KINGDOM OF HEAVEN IS LIKE UNTO A MAN SEEKING GOODLY PEARLS ; WHO WHEN HE HAD FOUND ONE PEARL OF GREAT PRICE, WENT AND SOLD ALL THAT HE HAD, AND BOUGHT IT.

11. In and with the Pall is conferred[2] the plenitude of the Episcopal Office. Hence it cometh that the Metropolitan may neither call a council, nor consecrate the Chrism, nor ordain clergy in his province, nor consecrate Bishops, nor dedicate Churches, nor take unto himself the title of Archbishop,[3] until he have been honoured therewith ; although there be some

---

[1] S. Matth. xiii. 45, 46.

[2] *Confertur*, v.l. *confortatur* (so latest ed.) which is perhaps better, as it is of course needless to say that the virtue of the Pall is purely *jurisdictive* and not *sacramental*, making the Bishop no more a Bishop, strictly speaking, than he was before.

[3] Nor that of Patriarch or Primate, nor have his Cross borne before him, not even though he be consecrated, nor even though he may have had another Pall in another Province. See, for this and remainder of Section, *Pontificale*, Pars I. Tit. xiv. ' De Pallio,' §§ v. viii. &c.

,who say that if he be invited outside his own province, he might confer Holy Order as a simple Bishop, without the Pall. Some there be, again, who affirm that a Bishop, even though he be such an one as may use the Pall, may not grant permission to an Archbishop of another province to wear the Pall in his diocese, unless the said Palled Bishop be an exempt; and that even an Archbishop may not do the like in his province, unless the Archbishop invited have special privilege of wearing the Pall outside his own province if he be so invited. But these be points rather of rigorous order than of courtesy; nor, save thou look upon the matter curiously, does the case of an exempt Palled Bishop seem to differ greatly from one not exempt.[1]

12. But one Metropolitan may not officiate with the Pall of another, nor by the same count may he be buried therein, but only in his own; nevertheless he who hath been Palled, if he have been translated unto another Church, is buried with the Pall granted unto him in his second place.[2] Nor may he who hath been Palled, if he be translated unto another Church, make use

---

[1] The passage seems corrupt.

[2] And if he be buried outside his own province, he may be buried with his own Pall; but not *wearing* it; it must be placed, folded, under his head. *Caer. Ep.* I. c. xvi. *in fine.*

there of the Pall .wherewith he was invested in
his former Church ; for the Pall is granted, not
in respect of persons only, but of place as well.
Hence it followeth that he may not wear it outside the province assigned unto him.   Moreover,
if anyone resign the Archbishoprick, he may no
longer wear the Pall.   Nor, again, may any
wear the Pall, save in Church, and at the
Church's offices ; thus if it should fall to his lot
to go out of Church in procession, or to preach,
or for any the like purpose, he shall not go out
with the Pall.

13. The use of the Pall is forbidden by rule,
save upon solemn Feasts, and such occasions as
may be contained among the privileges of each
several Church.   And the Festivals are as
followeth :—

    The Nativity of our Lord.
    Saint Stephen.
    Saint John.
    The Circumcision.
    The Epiphany.
    Palm Sunday.
    Maundy Thursday.
    Holy Saturday.
    The Three Days of the Resurrection.[1]

    [1] Easter Sunday, Monday, and Tuesday.

The Ascension.

Pentecost.

The Feast of Saint John Baptist.

The Feast of All Apostles.[1]

The Four Festivals of Blessed Mary.[2]

Saint Michael.

All Saints.

Saint Martin, Peer of the Apostles.[3]

Also[4] upon the principal Feasts of the Church honoured with the Pall[5]; and at

---

[1] Formerly May 1, the present Feast of SS. Philip and James. Micrologus (eleventh century) says that on that day ' inuenitur in Martyrologiis siue in Sacramentariis festiuitas SS. Phil. et Jac., *et omnium Apostolorum*.' This Commemoration was also associated, and more naturally, with the Feast of SS. Peter and Paul (June 29); and it is to this day observed upon the morrow of that Feast in the Greek Church, and called ' σύναξις τῶν δώδεκα 'Αποστόλων.'

[2] *I.e.* Purification (February 2), Annunciation (March 25), Assumption (August 15), and Nativity (September 8).

[3] Durandus says elsewhere (L. vii. ' De B. Martino ') that this name was given to S. Martin, not so much on account of the multitude of his miracles, as on account of one miracle, which the reader will find in Ch. iii. of this work, p. 31, n. 1.

[4] And now upon Corpus Christi Day, the Thursday after Trinity Sunday. Durandus does not include this, because it was not yet a regular Feast of the Church when he wrote the *Rationale* (about A.D. 1290). It was decreed as a Festival by Pope Urban IV. in 1264, but, Urban dying, it lapsed until his Bull was promulgated and confirmed at the Council of Vienne in 1311; and did not come into general observance until even later.

[5] *I.e.* the Metropolitan Church, or Cathedral.

The Dedication of Churches.

The Consecration of Bishops.[1]

The Ordination of Clergy; and upon

The Anniversaries of the consecration of him that weareth the Pall.

By some are added the Sundays after Easter; but this latter is not the common use· I may also mention that wherever in his province there resteth the body of any Saint, upon the Feast of that Saint, and even upon the principal Festival of any place in his province, the Metropolitan may visit that place and may there wear the Pall and Sandals. But at the Burial of the Dead, and at the Solemnisation of Matrimony, these may not be worn, unless there be contained in a Privilege the express permission to do so. The Bishop of Ostia,[2] who consecrateth the Pope, weareth the Pall, as ordained by Marcus, Pope; and there be

---

[1] And of Virgins.

[2] Anastasius Bibliothecarius says of Marcus, Bishop of Rome (c. A.D. 336), 'Hic constituit, ut Episcopus Ostiensis, qui consecrat Episcopum Urbis (sc. Romae) Pallio uteretur, et ab eodem episcopo [*lege* episcopus] Urbis Romae consecraretur' (*Vit. Pontif.* 49). ['He appointed that the Bishop of Ostia should wear the Pall, and should consecrate the Pope.'] Ménard quotes from an ancient MS. at Corbey (of unknown date) an Order of Papal Consecration in which the Bishops of Alba, Portus, and Ostia took part.

certain Bishops beside, who do so by special
privilege.

14. Lastly it is to be noted, that the Roman
Pontiffs who were before Blessed Silvester are
depicted as having linen Palls wrapt around
their shoulders (for the Priest of the Law, too,
when he sacrificed, turned back the ends of
the Girdle over his shoulders). And this
signifieth that the jurisdiction and authority of
those said Popes, as set forth by the Pall, were
involved and straitened, being not free. But
Silvester, and they that came after him, have had
power free and untrammelled; wherefore the
stripes of their Palls are represented as hanging
open and outspread behind and before. Another
reason why these stripes, which denote cares
and anxieties (as is aforesaid) do hang down
without fold since the days of Pope Silvester,
may be this,—because the temporalities have
been granted unto him and to his successors,
which may not be had without anxiety and
carefulness.

It hath been said by Bruno, that the
Sovereign Pontiff weareth, beside the Vestments
afore mentioned, the Regnum and Purple; and
this not for any mystical reason, but because
the Emperor Constantine did hand over to

Blessed Silvester all the insignia of the Roman
Empire. Wherefore in great processions all
that pomp, which used to be made in honour of
the Emperors, is displayed in the person of
the Roman Pontiff; and the Pope himself is
crowned with the Imperial diadem.

CHAPTER XVIII

OF THE FOUR COLOURS WHICH THE CHURCH USETH IN HER VESTMENTS

1. Of the Colours which Holy Church useth.—2. Of the Seasons wherein White Vestments be used.—3. Of White Vestments at the Dedication of a Church.—4. Of the Seasons wherein Red Vestments be used.—5. Of Martyrdom and Virginity.—6. Of the Seasons wherein Black Vestments be used.—7. Of the seasons wherein Green Vestments be used.—8. Unto these four all other Colours may be referred. 9. Of the Seasons wherein Violet Vestments be used.—10. Of the meaning thereof.

1. THERE be four principal colours, wherewith the Church doth make distinction in her sacred Vestments according to the propers of the seasons: namely, white, red, black, and green. For in the Vestments of the Law, too, we read that four colours were used, fine linen, purple, blue, and scarlet; of the which I purpose to treat in the following chapter. The Roman Church useth also violet and yellow, as shall be noted hereafter.

2. White Vestments are to be used at the times following :—

Upon the Feasts of holy Confessors, and Virgins who are not Martyrs, by reason of their integrity and innocence. For HER NAZARITES WERE WHITER THAN SNOW[1]; and THEY SHALL WALK WITH ME IN WHITE,[2] FOR THEY ARE VIRGINS, AND SHALL FOLLOW THE LAMB WHITHERSOEVER HE GOETH.[3]

For the same reason white is to be used upon the Festivals of the Angels, of whose brightness the Lord saith unto Lucifer,[4] WHERE WAST THOU WHEN THE MORNING STARS SHOUTED FOR JOY?

Upon all Feasts of Mary, Holy Mother of God.

Upon the Feast of All Saints (although there be some who use red at this time, as shall be further noted below).

---

[1] Lam. iv. 7.   [2] Rev. iii. 14.

[3] *Ibid.* xiv. 4.   Neale and Webb, who have given an epitome of this Chapter in their *Symbolism of Churches,* quote here the beautiful words of Laevinus Torrentius in his hymn on the Holy Innocents :—

'Ergo supremi parte coeli, lactea qua lucidum fulget via,
 Qua picta dulci stillat uva nectare, et nectar exhalant rosae,
 Laeti coronis luditis, et insignium mixti puellarum choris
 Sacrum canentes itis agnum candido quacunque praecedat
   pede.'

[4] Rather, to Job (Job xxxviii. 7).

Upon the principal Feast of S. John, Evangelist.[1]

Upon the Conversion of S. Paul.

Upon the Enthronement of S. Peter,[2] whereof I will speak again.

From the Vigil of our Lord's Nativity to the Octave of Epiphany inclusively, save only upon such Feasts of Martyrs as occur between.[3]

Upon the Nativity of our Saviour, and also of His Forerunner, for that both were born pure, that is, without original sin. For THE LORD RIDETH UPON A SWIFT CLOUD,[4] which is to say that He took Flesh unspotted of sin, and COMETH INTO EGYPT,[5] that is, into the world; according to that which the Angel spake unto the Virgin, THE HOLY GHOST

---

[1] *I.e.* December 27, his ' Deposition '; not May 6, 'S. John before the Latin Gate,' the day of his deliverance from the boiling oil.

[2] Called *Cathedra S. Petri Antiochiae,* or ' S. Peter's Chair at Antioch,' a Double, which occurs on February 22. It is explained as commemorating S. Peter's seven years' episcopate at Antioch (Leo, *Ep.* 119) where he had raised the son of Theophilus of Antioch from the dead, and converted the people; in consequence whereof they built a Church there, with a lofty throne in it, wherein they placed the Apostle, that he might be seen and heard by all. The Enthronement of S. Peter at Rome (Cath. S. Petri Romae) is in the Roman Calendar celebrated on January 18.

[3] S. Stephen, Holy Innocents, and S. Thomas of Canterbury.

[4] Is. xix. 1.   [5] *Ibid.*

SHALL COME UPON THEE, AND THE POWER
OF THE HIGHEST SHALL OVERSHADOW THEE.[1]
And John, even if thou hold him to have been
conceived in sin, was nevertheless sanctified in
the womb, as saith the Prophet, BEFORE THOU
CAMEST FORTH OUT OF THE WOMB I SANCTI-
FIED THEE[2]; and the Angel spake unto
Zachary concerning him, HE SHALL BE FILLED
WITH THE HOLY GHOST EVEN FROM HIS
MOTHER'S WOMB.[3]

White is used, again, in the Epiphany, by
reason of the brightness of the star which led
the Magi, as saith the Prophet,[4] THE GENTILES
SHALL COME TO THY LIGHT, AND KINGS TO
THE BRIGHTNESS OF THY RISING.

At Hypapante,[5] in honour of the purity of
Mary, who at that time according to the song
of Symeon did offer A LIGHT TO LIGHTEN THE
GENTILES.[6]

Upon Maundy Thursday, by reason of the
consecration of the Chrism,[7] for soul's cleansing ;

---

[1] S. Luke i. 35.   [2] Jerem. i. 15.
[3] S. Luke i. 15.   [4] Is. lx. 3.
[5] *I.e.* the Purification of Our Lady ; so called by its Greek
name (ὑπαντάω, to meet), signifying the meeting of the B.V.M.
by Simeon and Anna in the Temple.   Lat. *Occursus Domini.*
[6] S. Luke ii. 32.
[7] On that day the Bishop blesses three kinds of oil : one for
Holy Unction ; another, for anointing candidates for Holy

for cleanness is commanded in especial by the Gospel read upon that day, wherein the Lord saith, HE THAT IS BATHED NEEDETH NOT SAVE TO WASH HIS FEET, BUT IS CLEAN EVERY WHIT.[1] And again, IF I WASH THEE NOT, THOU HAST NO PART WITH ME.[2]

Upon Holy Saturday, in the Office of the Mass, and from thence unto the Octave of the Ascension inclusively, at all Offices of the season ; save only upon Rogation Days, and upon such Feasts of Martyrs as occur between, whereof I will speak anon.

Upon the Feast of the Resurrection, because of the Angel, the witness of the Resurrection, the herald, who appeared CLOTHED IN A LONG WHITE GARMENT[3]; of whom saith Matthew, that HIS COUNTENANCE WAS LIKE LIGHTNING, AND HIS RAIMENT WHITE AS SNOW.[4] Also because children, who receive the New Birth at that time, are arrayed in white garments.[5]

Baptism ; and another, with balsam, called the Chrism, for the anointing of Altars, of Sovereigns, and of candidates for Baptism and Confirmation.
   [1] S. John xiii. 10.   [2] *Ibid.* v. 8.
   [3] S. Mark xvi. 5.   [4] S. Matth. xxviii. 3.
   [5] Alluding to the ancient custom of baptising on Easter Eve, because we are 'buried with Him in Baptism,' and rise again to newness of life. Upon the newly-baptised linen vestments called 'chrisoms' were placed.

Upon the Feast of the Ascension, by reason of the bright cloud in which Christ ascended; for TWO MEN STOOD BY THEM IN WHITE APPAREL, WHICH ALSO SAID, YE MEN OF GALILEE, WHY STAND YE GAZING UP INTO HEAVEN?[1]

3. At the Dedication of a Church. For note, that although at the consecration of a Bishop the colour of Vestments shall be such as agreeth unto the proper of the day, yet at the Dedication of a Church white Vestments be always used, whatever be the day of its solemnisation. The reason hereof is, that at the Consecration of a Bishop the Mass of the day is sung, but at the Dedication of a Basilica, the Mass of Dedication. For the Church is named with the name of a Virgin, according to that of the Apostle, I HAVE ESPOUSED YOU TO ONE HUSBAND, THAT I MAY PRESENT YOU AS A CHASTE VIRGIN TO CHRIST.[2] And of her the Bridegroom saith in the Canticles, THOU ART ALL FAIR, MY LOVE; THERE IS NO SPOT IN THEE.[3] Yet the Bishop himself who is consecrated weareth white Vestments, to denote that at all times HIS GARMENTS (that is, his life) MUST BE WHITE[4] (that is, without stain).

---

[1] Acts i. 10, 11.　　[2] 2 Cor. xi. 2.　　[3] Cant. iv. 7.
[4] Eccles. ix. 8.

And, lastly, white Vestments are used throughout the Octaves of such of the Feasts aforesaid as have Octaves, at all Offices wherein such Octaves are kept.

4. Red Vestments are used at the following times :—

Upon the Festivals of Apostles, Evangelists, and of Martyrs, by reason of the blood of suffering which they shed for Christ ; for THESE ARE THEY WHICH CAME OUT OF GREAT TRIBULATION [1] ; save only upon the Feast of the Holy Innocents, as shall be presently set forth.

Upon the Feast of that Holy Cross, whereon Christ shed His Blood for us ; as saith the Prophet, WHEREFORE ART THOU RED IN THINE APPAREL, LIKE HIM THAT TREADETH IN THE WINEFAT ? [2] But others say it is better to use white on that day, since it is the Feast, not of the Passion, but of the Invention [3] or Exaltation [4] of the Cross.

At Mass from the Vigil of Pentecost until the Sabbath following, inclusively ; because of the burning fire of the Holy Spirit, Who appeared upon the Apostles in tongues of fire ;

---

[1] Rev. vii. 14.   [2] Is. lxiii. 2.
[3] May 3, whereon S. Helena discovered the True Cross.
[4] September 14, whereon Heraclius the Emperor recovered it from Chosroës.

for THERE APPEARED UNTO THEM CLOVEN
TONGUES LIKE AS OF FIRE, AND IT SAT UPON.
EACH OF THEM.[1]   And according to the Pro-
phet, FROM ABOVE HATH HE SENT A FIRE IN
MY BONES.[2]   But although upon the Feast of
the Martyrdom of the Apostles Peter and Paul
red be used, yet upon the Conversion of Saint.
Paul, and upon the Enthronement of Saint
Peter, we wear white.   And though upon the
Nativity of Saint John Baptist white be worn,
yet is red used upon his Decollation.

5. And upon the Feast of a Saint who is
both Martyr and Virgin, the Martyrdom hath
the preference, for it is the sign of love in perfection ; as saith the Truth, GREATER LOVE HATH
NO MAN THAN THIS, THAT A MAN LAY DOWN
HIS LIFE FOR HIS FRIENDS.[3]

For this reason there be some who use red
Vestments in the Commemoration of All Saints,
but others use white, as doth the Roman
Church, for that not only on that day, but con-
cerning it, the Church saith that the Saints, as
according to John in the Apocalypse, will stand
BEFORE THE LAMB, CLOTHED WITH WHITE
ROBES, AND PALMS IN THEIR HANDS.[4]   The

---

[1] Acts ii. 3.   [2] Lam. l. 13.   [3] S. John xv. 13.
[4] Rev. vii. 9, part of the Epistle for the Day. Durandus
died on this day.

Bride saith also in the Canticles, MY BELOVED
IS WHITE AND RUDDY, THE CHIEFEST AMONG
TEN THOUSAND[1]; that is, He is white, in His
Confessors and Virgins, and red, in His Martyrs
and Apostles; for these are the roses, those the
lilies of the valley. They, on the other hand,
who wear red on All Hallows' Day, are
prompted by the thought that this Feast was
first instituted in honour of Martyrs only.[2] But
unto this it may be answered, that it was instituted in honour of the Blessed Virgin also;
and that nowadays the Church holdeth festival
on that day on behalf not of Martyrs only, but
of Confessors and Virgins also, according to
the institution of Gregory.

And lastly, Red is used throughout the
Octave of such of the Festivals foregoing as

---

[1] Cant. v. 10. Cp. Hymn at Lauds for a Virgin Martyr,
in Paris Breviary :—

> Liliis Sponsus recubat, rosisque ;
> Tu, tuo semper bene fida Sponso
> Et rosas Martyr, simul et dedisti
> Lilia Virgo.

[2] Pope Boniface IV., in the seventh century, dedicated on
May 11, in honour of the 'B.V.M. and All Martyrs,' the
Pantheon, a heathen temple formerly sacred to 'All Gods and
Goddesses.' On that day the Feast of S. Maria ad Martyres
was kept until the time of Gregory IV. (A.D. 835), when it was
transferred to November 1, our present All Saints' Day, because
the harvest was then gathered in.

have Octaves, whensoever the Office shall be of the Octave.

6. Black is worn upon the following :—

Upon Good Friday.

Upon days of affliction [1] and fasting for sin, and upon Rogation Days.

In barefoot processions which the Lord Pope maketh.

In Masses for the dead.

From Advent Sunday unto the Vigil of the Nativity.

From Septuagesima unto Holy Saturday. For the Bride saith in the Canticles,[2] I AM BLACK BUT COMELY, O YE DAUGHTERS OF JERUSALEM, AS THE TENTS OF KEDAR, AS THE CURTAINS OF SOLOMON ; LOOK NOT UPON ME BECAUSE I AM BLACK, BECAUSE THE SUN HATH LOOKED UPON ME.

---

[1] The question of ancient colours is so difficult as to be almost hopeless to any but a specialist upon the subject. Durandus' period seems to have been transitional between the uses of black and violet, for in § 9 he proceeds to give violet as an alternative colour for black. The early Church doubtless regarded black with less strictness than we, and used it interchangeably with other sombre colours, such as 'color uiolaceus' or 'purpureus niger.' It appears also that in Durandus' time the tendency to differentiate the great day of Our Lord's Death from mere penitential seasons was becoming more marked.

[2] Cant. i. 5, 6.

Upon the Feast of the Holy Innocents
some do contend that black, some that red,
Vestments should be used. They who favour
black, allege the sadness of the day, how that
IN RAMA WAS THERE A VOICE HEARD, LAMEN-
TATION, AND WEEPING, AND GREAT MOURN-
ING, RACHEL WEEPING FOR HER CHILDREN,
AND WOULD NOT BE COMFORTED, BECAUSE
THEY ARE NOT[1]; and how for the same cause
the joyous hymns upon that day are hushed,[2]
and the Mitre without orfrey is brought. They
on the other hand who contend for red,
affirm that it is a day of martyrdom, in commemoration principally whereof the Church
saith, 'All the Saints cry out beneath the
Throne of God, Avenge our blood which is
poured forth, O Lord our God.'[3] (So also
upon Lactare Sunday, for the joy which the
Golden Rose[4] bespeaketh, the Bishop of Rome

[1] Jer. xxxi. 15 ; S. Matth. ii. 18 ; in substance the 'Com-
munio' of the day in the Roman Missal.

[2] The Gloria in Excelsis, Alleluia, and 'Ite Missa est' are
not said upon this day. But 'Credo' is said.

[3] See Rev. vi. 9, 10. An expansion of the Tract for the day.

[4] At the end of Mass on the Fourth Sunday in Lent the
Pope used to bless a rose full of musk and balsam, and present
it to some Christian sovereign. Fulk of Anjou (In 'Fragment.
Hist. Andegav.' in d'Acherii *Spicil.* Tom. X.) mentions this
ceremony in the eleventh century, and Durandus gives an
account of it in his day (*Rat.* Lib. vi. c. 53).

hath a Mitre adorned with the orfrey, but black
Vestments, by reason of the Lenten Fast.) But
the Roman Church useth violet Vestments
upon Holy Innocents' Day, when it falleth
upon other than Sunday[1]; and upon its
Octave, always red.

7. The colour that remaineth is Green, and
this is used at the following times :—

Upon ferial and common days, because this
colour is a kind of mean betwixt white, and
black, and red.

And especially between the Octave of
Epiphany and Septuagesima, and between Pentecost and Advent, whensoever the Office shall
be of the Sunday. For this colour is exprest
in the words, CAMPHIRE WITH SPIKENARD,
SPIKENARD AND SAFFRON.[2]

8. And unto these four colours thou mayest
refer all the others: namely, unto red, scarlet ;
unto black, violet ; unto white, fine linen ; and
unto green, yellow.[3] Nevertheless according
to some the rose belongeth unto Martyrs, the
yellow crocus to Confessors, and the lily unto

---

[1] And red, when it does fall on Sunday ; but red *always* on
its Octave, on whatever day it fall.

[2] Cant. iv. 13, 14.

[3] This passage seems corrupt and obscure.

Virgins. And of colours I will treat also at the end of the following chapter.

9. It is not unmeet to use Violet at those seasons whereunto black belongeth. Thus the Roman Church useth violet from the first Sunday of Advent unto Mass on the Vigil of the Nativity inclusively, and from Septuagesima unto Mass on Easter Eve exclusively of the latter,[1] whensoever the Office is of the season ; except upon Maundy Thursday[1] and Good Friday.[2] But upon such Saints' Days as occur in Lent and Advent neither black nor violet is to be worn. And be it understood that upon Holy Saturday violet is to be worn at every office[3] which hath place before Mass ; with this exception, that the Deacon who blesseth the Paschal Candle, and the Subdeacon[4] who serveth him, are vested respectively in a Dalmatic and Tunicle of white, for that such

---

[1] Because white is used then.   [2] Which is always black.

[3] These are the beautiful ceremonies of the Blessing of the New Fire and of the Paschal Candle, the reading of the Twelve Prophecies, the Blessing of the Font, the Baptisms, and the singing of the Litanies. During all these the Priest is vested in violet ; but the Deacon wears white for the first two. Then all put on white Vestments for Mass.

[4] The Missal says ' in Benedictione Cerei in Sabbato Sancto . . . . Diaconus *solus* utitur Albo.' But this inclusion of the Subdeacon is probably a slip on Durandus' part ; for, a few lines lower, he says ' Subdiaconus uero non mutat uestes.'

Blessing of the Candle, as also the Mass itself, hath respect unto the Resurrection. But after the Blessing done, the Deacon layeth aside his Dalmatic, and putting on a violet folded-chasuble keepeth the same even until the beginning of Mass. But the Subdeacon changeth not his Vestments.

Some, again, wear white Vestments upon Palm Sunday in the Procession and at the Blessing of Palm-branches, and during the singing of the Gospel and of the *Gloria laus et honor*, by reason of the gladness of the honour offered unto Christ, which is commemorated in those parts of the Office. But the Roman Church useth always violet at those times; as also in the Procession before Mass on the Feast of the Purification, because that Office bringeth to mind the anxious expectation of Symeon, and savoureth of the Old Testament.

10. The Roman Church useth Violet also upon the Ember Days of September, and upon such Vigils of Saints' Days as are Fasts, when Mass shall be of the Vigil. Also upon Rogation Days, and at the Mass of Litanies upon the Feast of Saint Mark.[1] For when we fast, we

---

[1] The 'Greater Litany,' ordered by S. Gregory the Great on the Feast of S. Mark (April 25) to avert God's wrath on the

do buffet and crucify the flesh, that being livid with stripes it may be conformed unto the stripes which Christ suffered, WITH WHOSE STRIPES WE ARE HEALED[1]; and in token hereof we do at times of fasting use violet, which is pale, and as it were of the hue of stripes.

It may be noted that at the Feast of Easter there are Veils[2] of three colours placed upon the Altar.

occasion of a pestilence.   The 'Lesser Litany' is used on the Rogation Days.

[1] Is. liii. 5.

[2] 'In some Churches at Easter the Altar is arrayed in precious palls, and in veils of three colours, red, pale (*sub-album*) and black; and these denote three seasons.   After the first Lection and Responsory finisht, the black one is taken away, which denoteth the time before the Law; after the second, the pale veil, the time under the Law; and after the third, the red, the day of grace, wherein we have access unto the Holy of Holies through the Passion of Christ' (*Ra/.* Lib. I. c. 'De Picturis').

CHAPTER XIX

OF THE VESTMENTS OF THE LAW, OR OF
THE OLD TESTAMENT [1]

1. Of the Vestments of the Law, according unto History. And first, of the Four which were common unto all Priests. 2, 3, 4, 5. Of those that were peculiar to the High Priest. 6. Of the Vestments of the Law, according unto Allegory. 7. Of the same, according unto Parable.—8. Of the Linen Coat.—9. Of the Girdle.—10. Of the Long Tunic.—11. Of the Ephod.—12. Of the Breastplate.—13. Of its fashioning, and of Urim and Thummim.—14. Of that which standeth in the stead of the Breastplate to-day.—15. Of the Mitre. 16. Of the Golden Plate.—17. Of the Making and Colours of the Vestments of the Law.—18. Of the Pope: and wherefore he weareth red.—19. Of the reason why he beareth all the Imperial insignia.

1. NOW seeing that human weakness comprehendeth the meaning of things the less fully, if it be ignorant essentially of the things themselves; we will say a few words upon the Vestments of the Law, unto the dispelling of

---

[1] The whole of this Chapter should be read *pari passu* with Ex. xxviii. (Vulg.) and with Josephus, *Ant.* Lib. iii. c. 7, from which it is closely borrowed in great part.

this blind ignorance whereof I speak.   And let us treat them, first, according to history[1] ; secondly, according to allegory ; and thirdly, according to parable.

First, then, as speaking historically, thou must know that according to the Mosaic Law there were four Vestments common both to the lesser Priests and to the High Priest himself; and of these we read in the twenty-eighth chapter of Exodus.[2]

The first was called *Manascasim*,[3] that is, linen Breeches, wove of fine twined linen, worn for that purpose whereof we read in the

---

[1] 'Secundum historiam, allegoriam, tropologiam.'   The distinction between the two latter is hard to reproduce succinctly.   Perhaps the above comes nearest ; for Durandus, in interpreting the ancient Vestments ' *allegorice*,' finds in them a representation of the material Universe ; and ' *tropologice*,' a picture of faith and morals.   Elsewhere (*Rat.* Proeme, 9, 10, 11), he quotes S. Jerome as saying that ' Scripture must be studied in three ways : (i.) according to the letter ; (ii.) after ' allegory,' *i.e.* the spiritual meaning ; and (iii.) according to the blessedness of the future.'   And he defines allegory as ' when one thing is said and another meant,' and tropology as ' an injunction unto morality.'   We are reminded of Origen's ' literal, moral, and mystical.'

[2] All are given in *vv.* 40 and 42.

[3] I shall quote the Hebrew words as spelt by Durandus.   It must be remembered, as Dr. Neale reminds us, that in his time Greek and Hebrew were little known in Europe.   The word he intends here is *michnasim*, from *canas*, to hide.

twentieth chapter of Exodus,[1] THOU SHALT
NOT GO UP BY STEPS UNTO MINE ALTAR,
THAT THY NAKEDNESS BE NOT DISCOVERED
THEREON.

The second was the *Cathemone*,[2] or the
Linen Coat, which we call the Subuncula,[3] or
Albe; but Moses calleth it *Abaneth*[4]; and the
Hebrews, when they departed from Babylon,
called it *Emissanea*. This was of fine linen,
and twofold.

The third was Balteus, that is, the Zone or
Girdle; this was about four fingers in breadth,
and was netlike, so as to resemble a viper's
skin; and it was wove of fine linen, scarlet,
purple, and blue, which were symbols of the four
elements.

The fourth was the Tiara, which the Hebrews
named *Mamphie*, and which we call Bonnet,[5] or

---

[1] Ex. xx. 26; Ezek. xliv. 18.

[2] *Cethoneth* (χιτών). This Vestment did not differ in the
High Priest and the lesser Priests. It was a long tunic like a
cassock, worn, according to Josephus, next the skin, and
reaching to the feet, with close sleeves (*Ant.* iii. 7, § 2); uni-
form in colour, and diapered (Ex. xxviii. 39, ' embroidered ').

[3] *Subucula*, Lat. for a man's under-garment.

[4] Doubtless Durandus means *Abnet*. But that was the name
of the Girdle, not of the Linen Coat. Durandus seems to have
inadvertently transferred Josephus's *Abnet* and *Emissanea* (both
of which Josephus applies to the Girdle) to the wrong Vestment.

[5] I have adopted the word which in the E. V. distinguishes

Mitre ; this, in the case of the lesser Priests,
differed for the most part from the High
Priest's Mitre, resembling in shape a round
helm.

2. Over and above these four common Vestments, there were four worn by the High Priest,
peculiar to him.

The first was the blue Robe, called in
Hebrew *Vethit*,[1] in Greek Poderes, in Latin
Talaris, that is, the garment that reacheth unto
the feet ; it had for its fringes pomegranates
and eighty golden bells disposed alternately,
that the sound of the latter might be heard

the headgear of the Priests from that of the High Priest.   The
former wore caps of a simple make, probably cup-shaped, called
migbaoth, or turbans.

[1] Properly, *meil*. It is called in the Bible the *Robe of the
Ephod* ('Tunica Superhumeralis,' Ex. xxviii. 31 *et seq.*).   A
very simple Vestment, reaching perhaps a little below the knees,
and all of blue.   Its subdued colour must have been seen above
and below the Ephod, as a background to its brilliant hues.   A
round hole at the top, hemmed to prevent tearing, admitted the
head.   The bells which hung between pomegranates from its
lower hem, like all ritual accessories, had a twofold meaning—
Godward and manward.   For in the first place they were a witness
to God that the Priest was wearing his Divinely-appointed Vestments, 'that he die not.'   And secondly, being heard by the
people outside the Tabernacle, they conveyed to them the
knowledge of their unseen Priest's intercession on their behalf,
and so acted, like our own Sanctus Bells, as a spur to their
devotion.

when the High Priest entered into the sanctuary, 'that he die not.' [1]

3. The second was the Ephod, or Super-humeral.[2] This was wove of the four colours aforesaid, with gold ; it was sleeveless,[3] after the manner of an undergarment, having an opening in the breast of a span square, wherein was fastened the Breastplate, being of the same size. And upon the upper part of the Ephod, that is, upon its shoulders, were set in golden ouches [4] two onyx-stones, whereon were graven the names of the twelve sons of Israel, six on the one, and six on the other. We read that Samuel and David [5] were clad with an ephod ; but this was of linen, and was properly called *Ephotar.*

[1] Ex. xxviii. 35.

[2] *I.e.* the ' Vestment worn over the shoulders.' (LXX ἐπωμίς). It was the distinctive Vestment of the High Priest (Ex. xxviii. 6–12). *Ephod* (from *aphad*, ' to put on ') is Hebrew for Vestment, just as our Chasuble is called ' the Vestment.' It was woven of blue, purple, scarlet, and fine twined linen ; and seems to have consisted of two pieces back and front, joined by shoulder-straps, somewhat after the manner of the modern French Chasuble. It had also what is called in Ex. xxviii. 8 a ' curious girdle,' *i.e.* a band, attached to it, which the High Priest fastened round his body when he put the Vestment on.

[3] Josephus says it had sleeves (*Ant.* iii. 7, § 5). But it may have altered by his time.

[4] *I.e.* settings of gold wire woven in a sort of filagree-work.

[5] 1 Sam. ii. 18 ; 2 Sam. vi. 14.

4. The third, called in Hebrew *Heen*, in Greek Logion, and in Latin Rationale,[1] or Breastplate, was worn by the High Priest upon his breast. It was called the Breastplate of Judgment ; for there was a stone[2] therein, by whose brightness[3] he knew that God was favourable unto him. Now the Breastplate was four-square, being doubled, a span broad and long ; it was fashioned of the four colours fore-

[1] So Vulg., and Latin Fathers, in reference to its oracular use. Heb: *choshen*, from *chashan*, 'to be adorned.' LXX, Jesus the son of Sirach, Philo, Josephus, and Epiphanius all call it λογεῖον. It was 'a piece of cunning work' like the Ephod (Ex. xxviii. 15 *et seq.*), two spans long and one broad. This, folded lengthways (perhaps for use as a bag), made a square of a span. It must have been something like a burse.

[2] The Urim and Thummim. Many are the theories as to the nature of this oracle in the Breastplate. A passage in Philo (*Vit. Mos.* iii. 11) has given rise to the notion that they were two small images of precious stone, kept in the bag of the Breastplate (Ex. xxviii. 30). All that seems certain about them, however, is that they were visible objects bound up with the history of the Jews, and that they were the means of revealing God's will to the High Priest, perhaps upon some principle of casting lots. They do not seem to have been heard of after the time of David. Josephus, with a touch of pathos, remarks : 'Now this Breastplate left off shining two hundred years before I compiled this book, God having been displeased at the transgression of His laws.'

[3] Josephus seems to attribute the shining properties to the 'sardonyx' upon the right shoulder-piece of the Ephod, and even to the twelve stones set in the Breastplate. It is more probable that the oracular virtue was resident in two objects *within* the Breastplate itself.

going, with gold. And it had twelve stones,[1]
even four rows of stones. In the first row were
a sardius, a topaz, and an emerald. In the
second row, a carbuncle, a sapphire, and a jasper.
In the third, a ligure, an agate, and an amethyst.
In the fourth, a chrysolite, an onyx, and a beryl-
stone. And upon these were graven the names
of the twelve sons of Israel, every one with his
name, according unto the order of their birth;
and upon the Breastplate were inscribed also
these two words, URIM, THUMMIM,[2] that is,
Doctrine and Truth. And the Breastplate was
made fast at [3] its upper part unto the Ephod by

[1] Most of them of course defy accurate identification. Durandus gives a list identical with that of the Vulgate, and nearly
so with that of Josephus, except that the order of the latter
differs slightly.

[2] So LXX, and Syriac Version. But were these words *inscribed on* the Breastplate? The Vulgate rendering of Ex.
xxviii. 30, 'Pones in rationali Doctrinam et Veritatem,' would
seem to have conveyed this impression to Durandus. But
'pones' here surely = *insert* rather than *inscribe*; and it seems
more likely that the Urim and Thummim were things put into
the Breastplate than words written on it.—As to the meaning
of the words, different interpretations exist. LXX gives ἡ
δήλωσις καὶ ἡ ἀλήθεια; Symmachus, φωτισμοὶ καὶ τελειότητες.
Durandus, as usual, adheres to the Vulgate.

[3] In other words, the Breastplate had a ring at each corner
of its square; the two upper rings hung by twisted gold wire
from settings in the upper part of the shoulder-pieces of the
Ephod, under the onyx-stones; and the two lower rings, which
were out of sight, were fastened by blue laces or strings to two

two rings, unto which were attached two golden
chains, the other ends of the chains being
fastened into two ouches which were fixt
beneath the aforesaid onyx-stones to the Ephod;
and at its lower part also it was joined unto the
Ephod by the means of two other golden rings,
into which were fastened two strings or laces of
blue.

5. The fourth and last Vestment was that of
the head, to wit, the Tiara or Mitre [1]; this did
end in a point, and had a golden circlet, with
pomegranates and flowers; and from it there
did hang down upon the brow a Plate of gold,[2]
in the shape of an half-moon, whereon was
written *Anoth Adonai*, to wit, the Holy Name
of the Lord, the Tetragrammaton or Four-
lettered Name, whereof again below. And
this Plate, lest it should move when the High
Priest moved, was bound with a blue lace or

rings sewn into the lower ends of the shoulder-pieces of the
Ephod, just above that band for fastening it which was called
the 'curious girdle.' Thus the Breastplate was held quite
firmly in its place (Ex. xxviii. 13, 14, and 22-28).

[1] This seems to have been a sort of augmentation of the
'Bonnet' of the lesser Priests. Josephus makes it double, with
a golden crown polished, of three rows, one above another,
out of which rose a cup of gold, which resembled the herb
'saccharus' (*Ant.* iii. c. 7, § 6).

[2] Ex. xxviii. 36, 37.

M

ribband, plain to see, having its ends flowing loosely behind.

Now our own Bishop hath,—

In the stead of the Breeches, the Sandals.

For the Linen Coat he hath the Albe.

For the Girdle, the Girdle.

For the Robe of the Ephod, the Tunic.

For the Ephod, the Amice, or the Stole.

For the Breastplate, the Pall.

For the ancient Mitre or tiara, the Mitre.

For the Golden Plate, the Cross.

And of these Vestments certain have a different shape from those, but each hath the same notion as that other which it representeth.

6. Secondly, let us speak of the meaning of the aforesaid Vestments of the Law, according to allegory.

The High Priest, adorned with these Vestments, did represent as in a picture the whole of Creation. For the Breeches of fine linen did meetly signify the earth,[1] because fine linen cometh from the earth. The Girdle, with its laces and strings, denoted the ocean that

---

[1] Most of this 'allegorical' interpretation is taken from Philo and Josephus. Both were versed in Gentile lore, as the Western character of this mode of interpretation testifies. The latter makes the *Breastplate* symbolic of the earth, for 'that hath the middle place of the universe' (§ 7).

windeth round it. The blue Tunic, by its hue,
was the firmament; the Bells, the sound of the
thunder; the Pomegranates, the gleam of the
lightnings. The four Vestments of the lesser
Priest, and the four of the greater, represented
by their number the four parts of Man, the
Microcosm,[1] and the four parts of Nature, the
Macrocosm,[2] to wit, the four Temperaments, and
the four Elements. The Ephod, with its many
hues, was a picture of the starry heaven; the
gold interwove with the colours, the warmth of
life which penetrateth all things; and the two
onyx-stones were the sun and moon, or the two
hemispheres. The twelve pectoral jewels in the
Breastplate represented the twelve signs of the
zodiac; and the Breastplate itself, or Rationale,
being in the midst, did shew forth that *Ratio*[3]
or Law whereof all things on earth are full,
whereby they cleave in obedience unto things in
the heavens; yea, the law of the life of earth,
and of the seasons of heat and cold and the
temperate periods between them both, which

---

[1] The *little world*, i.e. Man.

[2] The *great world*, i.e. the Universe.

[3] An obscure and seemingly corrupt passage; but the general
sense is that all Nature moves by law, and that the laws which
operate on earth are regulated in their turn by the laws of the
heavenly bodies.

cometh down from the law of the courses of the heavenly bodies. The rings and chains and ouches signified the linking together of the elements, and temperaments, and seasons. The Mitre shadowed forth the vast vault of heaven; the Golden Plate upon it represented God presiding over all things. And all this allegory is confirmed by the authority of the eighteenth chapter of the Book of Wisdom,[1] wherein it is written, FOR IN THE LONG GARMENT, WHICH HE HAD, WAS THE WHOLE WORLD, AND IN THE FOUR ROWS OF THE STONES WAS THE GLORY OF THE FATHERS GRAVEN, AND THY MAJESTY UPON THE DIADEM OF HIS HEAD.

7. In the third place must be added the explication of the Vestments of the Law according to parable.

Now the following was the order wherein the Priest of the Law was wont to array himself in the Vestments.

Having first washed his hands and feet, he put on the Breeches, in token that the Priest, having cleansed his affections and works with the tears of penance, ought to put on Continence, that he might offer a sacrifice without

[1] Verse 24.

spot, sacred, acceptable unto God.[1]   But our own Bishop, for that he ought to have continence alway, putteth not on breeches for sacrifice, but Sandals, as though one might say, HE THAT IS BATHED[2] NEEDETH NOT SAVE TO WASH HIS FEET, BUT IS CLEAN EVERY WHIT.   For by the hands are signified works, according to that Scripture,[3] BLESSED BE THE LORD MY STRENGTH, WHO TEACHETH MY HANDS TO WAR, AND MY FINGERS TO FIGHT; and by the feet the affections, as it is written, SHAKE OFF THE DUST OF YOUR FEET.[4]   And it is to be noted, that the Priest did himself put on him the Breeches, which were a type of virginal continence: these, I say, for that virginity is a matter of counsel, not of commandment, he did put on with his own hand, in agreement with that of Paul to the Corinthians,[5] NOW CONCERNING VIRGINS I HAVE NO COMMANDMENT OF THE LORD ; BUT I GIVE MY JUDGMENT.   And

[1] From the prayer ' *Unde et memores* ' immediately after the Consecration in the Missal.   ' Hostiam puram, Hostiam sanctam, Hostiam immaculatam.'

[2] S. John xiii. 10.   The E. V. rendering, ' he that is washed,' loses all the force of the sentence.   ' Ὁ λελουμένος,' i.e. ' he that is bathed all over ' (λούω), ' οὐ χρείαν ἔχει εἰ μὴ τοὺς πόδας νίψασθαι,' i.e. ' needeth only to wash his feet ' (νίπτω) as when one comes in from a journey.

[3] Ps. cxliv. 1.   [4] S. Matth. x. 14.   [5] 1 Cor. vii. 25.

the Lord in the Gospel saith Himself, HE THAT
IS ABLE TO RECEIVE IT, LET HIM RECEIVE
IT.[1]   Also the Priests were wont to put on this
Vestment by turns,[2] because they were not held ·
bound to perpetual virginity, as are the ministers
of the New Testament; and for this reason,
according to some, there is no Vestment nowadays answering thereto.

8. Next, he put on the Linen Coat, in token
that the Priest ought to put on innocence, that
he do not unto others that which he would not
have them do unto him.   For linen by its whiteness doth signify innocence, as it is written,
LET THY GARMENTS BE ALWAYS WHITE.[3]

9. In the third place he girded him with the
Girdle, the type of Chastity, wherewith he must
be girt around the loins, that he might keep in
subjection the concupiscence of the flesh; as
saith the Truth, LET YOUR LOINS BE GIRDED
ABOUT, AND YOUR LIGHTS BURNING IN YOUR
HANDS.[4]   This Girdle, being woven of four
colours, as is aforesaid, did betoken that he
ought to bridle all motions that should arise
from the four temperaments, or from the four

---

[1] S. Matth. xix. 12.
[2] *Alternatim.*   The reader must interpret this as he may.
[3] Eccles. ix. 8.   [4] S. Luke xii. 35.

elements; as it is said in the last chapter of the Proverbs,[1] A VIRTUOUS WOMAN DELIVERETH GIRDLES UNTO THE MERCHANT; and in the eleventh chapter of Esaias,[2] RIGHTEOUSNESS SHALL BE THE GIRDLE OF HIS LOINS. For it is by righteousness that all such animal motions are restrained. The Girdle also did hang down even unto the feet, for that he must be clean, yea, even unto the end of his life.

10. The fourth Vestment he put on was the Robe, which reached unto the heel, meaning that he must put on Perseverance; for HE THAT ENDURETH UNTO THE END SHALL BE SAVED.[3] For by the heel, which is the end of the body, we understand Perseverance, as it is written, IT SHALL BRUISE THY HEAD, AND THOU SHALT BRUISE HIS HEEL.[4] For a fringe, too, there hung from the Robe pomegranates with golden bells; now the pomegranate signifieth work, and the golden bells, preaching: which two things must be combined in the Priest, that HE DIE NOT, entering in without them into the sanctuary before the Lord. For Jesus Himself BEGAN BOTH TO DO AND TEACH,[5] leaving unto Priests AN EXAMPLE,   .

---

[1] Prov. xxxi. 24.   [2] Is. xi. 5.   [3] S. Matth. x. 22.
[4] Gen. iii. 15.   [5] Acts i. 1.

THAT THEY SHOULD FOLLOW HIS STEPS; WHO
DID NO SIN, that righteousness might be found
in their lives, NEITHER WAS GUILE FOUND IN
HIS MOUTH,[1] that in their preaching truth
might be found.

By the bells, again, we understand the
preacher's voice, that the Priest provoke not by
his silence the judgment of Him, Who being
above seeth all things; and the pomegranates
are the pattern of a good life, or the spirit of
martyrdom, because by fruit of this kind the
sick are refreshed. According to Gregory,[2] the
Priest must die, if on going in or out his sound
be not heard; which is to say, that he bringeth
upon himself the wrath of Him that judgeth in
secret, if he walk without the sound of preaching: and with this it agreeth well that he should
have bells, as we read, fastened unto his Vestments. Moreover, what are we to understand
by the Priest's Vestments, save righteous works,
according unto that of the Prophet, LET THY
PRIESTS BE CLOTHED WITH RIGHTEOUSNESS?
wherefore the bells cleave unto his Vestments,
that his very works may proclaim, as it were

[1] 1 S. Pet. ii. 21, 22.
[2] From this point, down to the words 'his life's way,'
Durandus is quoting from S. Gregory's *Pastoral*, Part II. c. iv.
(or xv.).

with tongues, his life's way. And the bells are joined with pomegranates, because these latter signify the unity of the Faith; for as in the pomegranate many seeds within are united together beneath one rind without, so the innumerable peoples of Holy Church are all overspread with the Unity of the One Faith, albeit they have a diversity of merit within.

11. The fifth Vestment he put on was the Ephod, which he placed over his shoulders, to shew that the High Priest ought to put on patience, that IN HIS PATIENCE HE MIGHT POSSESS HIS SOUL [1]; for it is upon the shoulders that we carry burthens, as it is written, HE BOWED HIS SHOULDER TO BEAR, AND BECAME A SERVANT UNTO TRIBUTE.[2] And it had the two shoulder-pieces thereof joined at the two edges thereof, signifying that the High Priest ought to have the ARMOUR OF RIGHTEOUS- NESS ON THE RIGHT HAND AND ON THE LEFT,[3] that he be not puffed up with well- being, nor cast down with reverses. Also were there two onyx-stones fastened into the shoulders thereof, whereon were graven the twelve names of the children of Israel, six on the one, and six on the other; and by these two

[1] S. Luke xxi. 19.   [2] Gen. xlix. 15.   [3] 2 Cor. vi. 7.

stones were represented Truth and Singleness
—Truth, by their brightness, and Singleness by
their solidity ; and the names of the children
of Israel were holy desires and works of righteousness, as it is written, 'Cursed is the man
that hath not left seed in Israel.' The number
six also doth denote perfection, for that on the
sixth day God FINISHED THE HEAVENS AND
THE EARTH, AND ALL THE HOST OF THEM.[1]
Thus the graving of the six names. of the
children of Israel on the one stone, and six on
the other, was a sign that the desires and works
of the Priest ought not to stand in the LEAVEN
OF MALICE AND WICKEDNESS, BUT IN THE
UNLEAVENED BREAD OF SINCERITY AND
TRUTH ;[2] that his intention be informed with
Singleness, and his end with Truth.

Gregory, in his Pastoral Letter,[3] saith that
they were bidden to make the Ephod of gold,
and blue, and purple, and twice-dyed scarlet,
and fine twined linen, for the shewing forth that
great diversity of virtues, wherewith the life of
the Priest should shine. And in his garments
it is gold that gleameth forth above all things,

---

[1] Gen. ii. 1.   [2] 1 Cor. v. 8.
[3] From here to the end of the Section is a selective quota-
tion from S. Greg. *Pastor*. Pt. II. c. iii. (or xiv.).

in token that in his life the understanding of
wisdom must shine out before all. And to this
is added blue, which gleameth in the hue of
heaven, that all things through which he maketh
way by his understanding may not minister
unto earthly men-pleasing, but may soar up
into the love of heavenly things ; lest while he
is unwisely taken up with the praises of himself,
he himself become void of the understanding
of truth. With the gold and the blue there is
also purple mingled, that the heart of the Priest,
while it hath hope concerning those lofty things
which he preacheth, may repress in itself the
suggestions of evil, and may as it were by a
royal authority refute them. Again, to the gold
and the blue, the fine linen and the purple, was
added scarlet twice-dyed, that before the eyes
of Him Who judgeth the hearts the excel-
lencies of all his virtues might be adorned with
the ornaments of Charity ; and that all those
merits in him which glitter before the eyes of
men, might be kindled in the sight of the
Secret Judge with the flame of an inner love.
For this Charity, that a man should love both
God and his neighbour, doth gleam as it were
with a double tinge. But when the mind
inclineth unto the precepts of Charity, it

remaineth that one buffet the flesh by Abstinence ; wherefore unto the twice-dyed scarlet fine
twined linen is added. For fine linen cometh
from the earth, with its radiant whiteness ;
what meaneth it, therefore, but the body's
chastity, so white with her comely pureness ?
and it is also twisted, ere it be inwoven with the
beauty of the Ephod ; because it is when the
flesh is wearied with fasting, that Chastity is
brought unto her whiteness clean and perfect.
For when amongst the other virtues the body's
discipline flourisheth, it is as though, amidst the
varied beauty of the Ephod, the fine twined
linen shewed its gleam.[1]

12. The sixth Vestment was the Breastplate
or Rationale, which was to say that the High
Priest must put on discretion, whereby he may
distinguish between light and darkness, between
the right hand and the left ; for light hath no
fellowship with darkness, neither CHRIST WITH
BELIAL.[2] This Breastplate also was four-square,
shewing that he must make distinction between
four things, namely, between truth and falsehood, that he swerve not in believing ; and

[1] A passage, and indeed a whole Section, of remarkable
beauty in he original.
[2] Cor. vi. 14, 15.

between good and evil, that he swerve not in
doing.   Double also it was, for that there were
two on whose behalf he must see clearly, to
wit, on his own behalf, and on his people's;
lest, the blind leading the blind, both should
fall into the ditch.   And it had four rows of
precious stones, because he must have four
Cardinal Virtues, namely, Justice, Fortitude,
Prudence, and Temperance; and in each row
it had three stones, for that he should have,
first, Faith, Hope, and Charity; secondly,
Modesty, Gentleness, and Kindness; thirdly,
Peace, Mercy, and Liberality; and fourthly,
Vigilance, Carefulness, and Long-suffering.
For precious stones are virtues, according to
that scripture, that one buildeth GOLD, SILVER,
AND PRECIOUS STONES.[1]

13. Two chains also it had of purest gold,
attached thereto each in his place, and themselves fastened into two ouches, signifying that
the High Priest ought to have two affections of
love, that is, unto God and his neighbour;
whereof we are taught, THOU SHALT LOVE THE
LORD THY GOD WITH ALL THY HEART, AND
THY NEIGHBOUR AS THYSELF.[2]   For as gold
taketh above all metals the pre-eminence, so

----

[1] 1 Cor. iii. 12.   [2] S. Luke x. 27.

Charity excelleth all virtues, as saith the Apostle[1] concerning it, THE GREATEST OF THESE IS CHARITY. The two ouches, into which the chains were fastened, were Intention and Consummation, that he should love God and his neighbour OUT OF A PURE HEART, AND OF A GOOD CONSCIENCE, AND OF FAITH UN-FEIGNED,[2] and also for the sake of blessedness ; loving God for his own sake, and his neighbour for God's. And this Breastplate of Judgment which Aaron wore, and whereon were inscribed the names of the twelve Patriarchs, was, as Gregory[3] saith, rightly called by this name ; because a ruler ought ever with subtle discrimination to judge betwixt good and evil : determining what things are meet to be diligently observed, and by whom, and at what time, and after what manner ; and not to seek his own, but to deem that the good of others agreeth best unto his own weal.   Thus in the Book of Exodus[4] it is written, AND THOU SHALT PUT IN THE BREASTPLATE OF JUDGMENT THE URIM AND THE THUMMIM ; AND THEY SHALL BE UPON AARON'S HEART, WHEN HE GOETH IN

[1] 1 Cor. xiii. 13.   [2] 1 Tim. i. 5.
[3] From here to end of Section is quoted from S. Greg. *Pastor.* Pt. II. c. ii. (or xiii.).
[4] Ex. xxviii. 30.

BEFORE THE LORD: AND AARON SHALL BEAR
THE JUDGMENT OF THE CHILDREN OF ISRAEL
UPON HIS HEART BEFORE THE LORD CON-
TINUALLY. Now, if a Priest 'bear the judg-
ment of the children of Israel upon his heart
before the Lord,' it is to say that he pleadeth
the cause of his flock before that Judge alone,
Who seeth the hearts of men.

14. Some, however, have said that there is
no Vestment to-day which answereth to the
Breastplate, because there is amongst·us no
plenty of precious stones. Yet it is after the
fashion of the Breastplate that the Bishop, at
his consecration, beareth the Text of the
Gospels [1] before his breast in the sight of all
the people ; for in this Text Doctrine and Truth
are put in writing ; and also ought the Bishop
to have in his heart the Truth of the Gospel,
and in his mouth its Doctrine as pertaineth to
the setting forth thereof. And this, it may
chance, is the reason why in certain Churches
the covers of the script of the Gospels are
embellished with gold, and silver, and precious

---

[1] The Book of the Gospels has long been held in the Latin
Church to be an integral part of the Consecration of a Bishop.
The Pontifical directs that it shall be placed by the Con-
secrator, in silence, upon the head and shoulders of the
Bishop-elect.

stones[1]; and there is also another reason,
for that in the Gospel there gleameth the
gold of wisdom, the silver of eloquence, and
the precious stones of wondrous works ; these
are the Bride's BORDERS OF GOLD, WITH STUDS
OF SILVER.[2]

15. The seventh and last Vestment was that
of the head, the Mitre or Tiara, which the High
Priest put on last of all, and which signified
humility ; whereof the Lord said, WHOSOEVER
EXALTETH HIMSELF SHALL BE ABASED, AND
HE THAT HUMBLETH HIMSELF SHALL BE
EXALTED.[3]   This he wore on his head, to shew
that the High Priest ought to bear humility in
his mind ; after the example of our Head, Who
saith, LEARN OF ME, FOR I AM MEEK AND
LOWLY IN HEART.[4]   For by the head we do
understand the mind, as it is written, ANOINT
THINE HEAD, AND WASH THY FACE.[5]   Again,
the Mitre, as worn by the lesser Priests, signified
Continence in the five senses ; but as worn by

[1] ' Leo III. caused to be made for the Apostle Peter, his
patron, a golden Book of the Gospels adorned round about
with jewels of marvellous size ' (V. Anast. in Vitaliano,
Leone III.).
[2] Cant. i. 11.   [3] S. Luke xiv. 11.   [4] S. Matth. xi. 29.
[5] Ibid. vi. 17.

the higher, Contemplation, whereunto they ought to be given.

16. From the front of the Mitre there hung down the Golden Plate, which was a figure of wisdom ; or, if thou wilt, it foreshadowed the Sign of the Cross, which is made in the Office of Confirmation.[1]   And upon this was graven tht Tetragrammaton, that is, the Four-lettered Name of the Lord; and the letters were Yod, He, Vav, He, that is, The Beginning of the Life of Passion.   Or, if one should speak more plainly, Christ, in Whose Name that High Priest did act, is the Beginning or Author of the Life of Passion, which is to say the Life that hath been restored through His Passion ; for BY HIS DEATH HE HATH DESTROYED OUR DEATH, AND BY HIS RISING TO LIFE AGAIN HATH RESTORED TO US EVERLASTING LIFE.[2]

17. Now all these Vestments were for the more part wove with work of varied colours, symbolising the variety of the virtues ; whereof saith the Psalmist,[3] UPON THY RIGHT HAND

---

[1] The Bishop, while he anoints the Candidate, says in the Roman rite, ‘I sign thee with the Sign of the Cross, and I confirm thee with the Chrism of salvation, in the Name of the Father, and of the Son, and of the Holy Ghost.’   That is why ‘ to confirm ’ is called in Latin *consignare*.

[2] From the Easter Preface in the Missal.   [3] Ps. xlv. 10.

N

DID STAND THE QUEEN IN A VESTURE OF
GOLD, WROUGHT ABOUT WITH DIVERS
COLOURS. And of four precious colours were
they wove, namely, purple, scarlet, fine linen,
and blue. The purple, the hue of kingly dignity, was the High-Priestly power; which needs
must walk a royal way, that it deviate neither
to the right hand nor to the left, that it bind
not the worthy, nor loose the unworthy. The
purple also signified water, because the worms
that wrought it dwelt in shells of the sea. The
scarlet, being of the colour of fire, signifieth the
doctrine of the High Priest, which must gleam
and burn like fire; wherefore also it is said to
have been twice-dyed. For it must gleam, in
promise, as that everyone who shall have left
HOUSE, OR FATHER, OR MOTHER, FOR HIS
NAME'S SAKE, SHALL RECEIVE AN HUNDRED-
FOLD, AND SHALL INHERIT EVERLASTING
LIFE[1]: and it must burn, in threatening, as
that EVERY TREE WHICH BRINGETH NOT
FORTH GOOD FRUIT SHALL BE HEWN DOWN,
AND CAST INTO THE FIRE.[2]

18. Hence it cometh that the Sovereign
Pontiff is ever seen to be clad with a red robe
without, while he weareth white garments

[1] S. Matth. xix. 29.   [2] *Ibid.* iii. 10.

within. For within he must be white with yet another whiteness, that is, Innocency and Charity ; and without he must be red as in token of compassion, that is, that he may shew himself ever ready to lay down his life for his sheep : for that he is Vice-gerent of Him Who made red His garments for all this world's sheep.

19. But by indulgence of Constantine,[1] Emperor, he may wear a purple cloak and a scarlet tunic, and all the robes of empire, the sceptre, the insignia, and ornaments. And whithersoever he goeth the Cross is borne in front of him, to shew that this Sign agreeth unto him more than unto all other ; as it is written by the Apostle, GOD FORBID THAT I SHOULD GLORY, SAVE IN THE CROSS OF OUR LORD JESUS CHRIST[2] ; that he may know it to be his duty to imitate the Crucified. Again, the scarlet twice-dyed in the High Priest's Vestments is Charity, which is as it were twice dyed, being coloured with the love of God, and the love of his neighbour.

By the fine linen, being of excellent white-

---

[1] See Chap. xiii., §§ 1 and 8, and Chap. xvii., § 14, with notes.
[2] 1 Tim. iii. 7.

ness, is signified the excellence of a good
report ; and it must be twined, that the High
Priest might have a good report both of them
that are within, and of them that are without,
as the Apostle hinteth.

And lastly, the blue, being of the colour of
the firmament, signified that serenity of conscience which the High Priest must have within
himself, according to that word of the Apostle,[1]
FOR OUR REJOICING IS THIS, THE TESTIMONY
OF OUR CONSCIENCE.

HERE ENDETH THE BOOK OF THE VEST-
MENTS OF THE CHURCH.

j

[1] 2 Cor. i. 12.

EPILOGUE

LET not any think that in the foregoing work the divine offices be sufficiently set forth, lest haply by praising man's work he rashly extenuate God's. For in the divine Office of the Mass there be wrapt up so many and great mysteries, that none shall have might to expound them, save he be instructed with an unction from the Holy. FOR WHO KNOWETH THE ORDINANCES OF HEAVEN, OR CAN EXPLAIN THE REASONS OF THEM UPON EARTH?[1] for he that prieth into their greatness shall be overwhelmed with the glory of it. But I, who cannot for the weakness of mine eyes look upon the wheeling sun in his brightness, have gazed, meseemeth, upon the majesty of so great mysteries as THROUGH A GLASS, DARKLY: and not penetrating into the interior of the palace, but sitting in the porch without, have done diligently, as I could, not sufficiently, as I

[1] Job xxxviii. 31.

would. For by reason of the innumerable and inevitable business of the Apostolic See,[1] pressing upon me daily, like a flood, and holding down the mind of one who would studiously rise to the contemplation of heavenly things; I, perplexed as it were, and entangled in divers inextricable knots, could not have full leisure as I would; wherefore I was able neither to dictate what I had thought out, nor compose what I ought. For the mind that is divided betwixt many things is devoted the less to each. Wherefore I crave not only a kindly reader, but a free corrector too; for I cannot gainsay that many things are inserted in this little work, which it were neither rash nor unjust to blame. But if aught praiseworthy be found therein, let it be ascribed entirely to Divine Grace, for EVERY GOOD GIFT AND EVERY PERFECT GIFT IS FROM ABOVE, AND COMETH DOWN FROM THE FATHER OF LIGHTS.[2] But let that which is unworthy be set down to human impotence, FOR THE CORRUPTIBLE BODY PRESSETH DOWN THE SOUL, AND THE EARTHLY TABERNACLE WEIGHETH DOWN THE MIND THAT MUSETH UPON MANY THINGS.[3]

---

[1] See ' Memoir of Durandus.'   [2] S. James i. 17.
[3] Wisdom ix. 17.

I have both collected from divers books and
commentaries, after the manner of the honey-
making bee, and from those thoughts which
Divine Grace hath held out to me, not without
fruit ; and this doctrine, flowing with inward
sweetness like the honey-comb, I have offered,
trusting in God's help, to those who are minded
to meditate on the divine offices ; looking for
this only guerdon among men for the great toil
which I have done, that they should pour forth
earnest prayers unto the most merciful Judge
for the assoiling of my sins.

HERE ENDETH HAPPILY THE RATIONALE
OF WILLIAM DURANDUS BISHOP OF
MENDE.

INDEX

THE CATHEDRAL BUILDERS

THE STORY OF A GREAT GUILD.

By LEADER SCOTT,

Hon. Mem. Accademia delle Belle Arti, Florence, Author of 'The Renaissance of Art in Italy,' 'Tuscan Studies,' 'Echoes of Old Florence,' 'Handbook of Sculpture,' &c.

About 80 Full-page Illustrations. In 1 vol. royal 8vo. cloth extra, 454 pp. Price 21*s.*

ALSO—A SPECIAL EDITION limited to One Hundred Copies, crown 4to. Printed on Imperial Hand-made Paper, the Illustrations printed on Japanese paper, price Three Guineas net.

The work is divided into four books, treating respectively of: I. Romano Lombard Architects; II. The First Foreign Emigrations of the Guild; III. Romanesque Architects; IV. Italian Gothic and Renaissance Architects.

WORKS BY THE REV. J. PATERSON SMYTH, LL.D.

1. HOW WE GOT OUR BIBLE. With Eight Illustrations. Crown 8vo. 1*s.*

The CHRISTIAN WORLD says:—'Gives an excellent and comprehensive account for popular reading of the ancient manuscripts of the Bible, and the versions of Wycliffe, Tyndale, and other translators.'

2. THE DIVINE LIBRARY: Suggestions How to Read the Bible. Crown 8vo. 1*s.*

'Can heartily recommend its suggestive pages to the careful attention of all Bible readers.'—BOOKSELLER.

3. HOW GOD INSPIRED THE BIBLE: Thoughts for the Present Disquiet. Crown 8vo. 2*s.* 6*d.*

4. THE OLD DOCUMENTS AND THE NEW BIBLE: An Easy Lesson for the People in Biblical Criticism. Illustrated. Crown 8vo. 2*s.* 6*d.*

Mr. Gladstone said of this volume:—'I have rarely seen the faculty of lucid exposition more conspicuously displayed.'

LONDON:

SAMPSON LOW, MARSTON & COMPANY, LIMITED,

St. Dunstan's House, Fetter Lane, E.C.

WORKS by the Rt. Rev. E. H. BICKERSTETH, D.D.
LORD BISHOP OF EXETER.

FROM YEAR TO YEAR. Original Poetical Pieces. New Edition. Small post 8vo. 5s. and 3s. 6d.; small post 8vo. calf or morocco, 10s. 6d.

THE FEAST OF DIVINE LOVE. New Edition. Small crown 8vo. 1s. 6d.

THE CLERGYMAN IN HIS HOME. Small 8vo. 1s.

EVANGELICAL CHURCHMANSHIP and ECLECTICISM. 8vo. 1s.

THE MASTER'S HOME CALL. Memorials of Alice Frances B. New Edition. 24mo. 1s.

MASTER'S WILL. A Sermon. 24mo. 1s.

OCTAVE OF HYMNS. Sewn, 3d.; with music, 1s.

SEPTETT OF MISSIONARY HYMNS. Crown 8vo. 1d.; with Tunes, 6d.

THE REEF, and other Parables. Illustrated. Square 8vo. 7s. 6d.; crown 8vo. 2s. 6d.

THE SHADOWED HOME AND THE LIGHT BEYOND. New Edition. 5s.

BICKERSTETH, EDWARD, D.D. Our Heritage in the Church; Papers written for Divinity Students in Japan. Crown 8vo. 5s.

COX, Rev. J. CHARLES, LL.D., F.S.A. Six Meditations on the Gardens of Scripture. Crown 8vo. 5s.

DIGGLE, Rev. CANON. Sermons for Daily Life. Crown 8vo. 5s.

HAWEIS, Rev. H. R. The Broad Church; or, What is Coming. Crown 8vo. 6s.

—————— Poets in the Pulpit. Crown 8vo. 6s. New Edition, 3s. 6d.

KEMPIS, THOMAS A. Daily Text-Book. Edited by W. E. WINKS. Crown 8vo. 2s. 6d.

—————— Imitation of Christ. A New Translation. Small 8vo. 2s. 6d.

ROGERS, C. Christian Heroes. Crown 8vo. gilt edges, 3s. 6d.; plain, 2s. 6d.

SAINTS AND THEIR SYMBOLS. New Edition. Crown 8vo. 3s. 6d.

SCHAFF, PHILIP. Christ in Song: Hymns of Immanuel, selected. New Edition. Crown 8vo. 6s.

TILESTON, MARY W. Daily Strength for Daily Needs. Selected by the Editor of 'Quiet Hours,' New Edition. Crown 8vo. 5s. and 3s. 6d.

LONDON:
SAMPSON LOW, MARSTON & COMPANY, LIMITED,
St. Dunstan's House, Fetter Lane, E.C.

www.ingramcontent.com/pod-product-compliance
Lightning Source LLC
Chambersburg PA
CBHW030825020726

47499CB00006B/2078